Alyson wanted to experience life. And she wanted to know what it was like to be held by a cowboy.

She played country music when no one was around. Cowboys were good at holding a woman. Unfortunately they were also good at breaking hearts.

She looked into his deep brown eyes and he winked.

Jason believed she was strong. He had let her prove it to herself by riding the mechanical bull.

Suddenly his hands moved to the clip at the back of her neck, and his hands wound themselves through her hair.

She could have stopped him, but she didn't. Instead she leaned toward him, breathing in the smell of soap and leather.

"I like it better this way," Jason whispered.

Alyson wanted to tell him to wait, to let this moment be one she'd never forget.

But before she could tell him, he held her close, and everything changed. She could think only about him, and nothing else.

Bull riding was nothing compared to that moment in the arms of a cowboy.

Books by Brenda Minton

Love Inspired

Trusting Him
His Little Cowgirl
A Cowboy's Heart
The Cowboy Next Door
Rekindled Hearts
Jenna's Cowboy Hero
The Cowboy's Courtship

BRENDA MINTON

started creating stories to entertain herself during hour-long rides on the school bus. In high school she wrote romance novels to entertain her friends. The dream grew and so did her aspirations to become an author. She started with notebooks, handwritten manuscripts and characters that refused to go away until their stories were told. Eventually she put away the pen and paper and got down to business with the computer. The journey took a few years, with some encouragement and rejection along the way—as well as a lot of stubbornness on her part. In 2006 her dream to write for the Steeple Hill Love Inspired line came true.

Brenda lives in the rural Ozarks with her husband, three kids and an abundance of cats and dogs. She enjoys a chaotic life that she wouldn't trade for anything—except, on occasion, a beach house in Texas. You can stop by and visit at her Web site, www.brendaminton.net.

The Cowboy's Courtship
Brenda Minton

Steeple
Hill®

Published by Steeple Hill Books™

STEEPLE HILL BOOKS

Steeple
Hill®

Recycling programs
for this product may
not exist in your area.

ISBN-13: 978-0-373-81464-0

THE COWBOY'S COURTSHIP

Copyright © 2010 by Brenda Minton

www.SteepleHill.com

Printed in U.S.A.

God be merciful to us, and bless us, and cause his face to shine upon us, That your way may be known on earth, your salvation among all nations.
—*Psalms* 67:1, 2

This book is dedicated to Doug, my real-life hero, because he's always there for me.

Chapter One

Until one month ago, Alyson Anderson hadn't even known that Etta Forester existed. Now she was sitting on a street just outside the small town of Dawson, Oklahoma, squinting through the windshield of her car at a yellow Victorian house with white gingerbread trim, shrubs that were pruned and flower gardens overflowing with pastel blooms.

She pulled her car into the driveway next to the house and parked. For a moment she sat there, not sure what her next move should be. Her hands shook on the steering wheel and her insides were quaking.

A mower reverberated in the quiet afternoon, and rolling down the window, Alyson could smell fresh-cut grass. She had lived in a lot of places, but never in a place like this.

Never in a place so quiet. She stepped out of her car, pulling off her sunglasses and clutching her purse under her arm. This was it, the moment she had been planning in her mind for nearly a week.

No, she'd been planning something like this for years. She had always planned to walk away someday. She'd been saving for this and waiting until the time was right, until no one else was depending on her.

Because she'd tried once before, but it had been a day on the road and she'd felt guilty because other performers, younger kids, had depended on her for guidance. No one else understood what they were going through, not like she did.

The mower she'd heard got louder.

A man walked around the corner of the house pushing it, not paying attention to her. She watched as he stopped and moved the garden hose, still not seeing her. She liked that, that he didn't notice her.

She liked watching him, a man in jeans, work boots and a stained T-shirt. A gardener perhaps. A gardener who looked a lot like England's Prince Harry, whom she'd met only twice. This man was older, but with the same light reddish-blond hair, the same tawny complexion.

He looked up, ending her quiet reflection. He killed the engine on the mower and paused, staring at her as if she was some type of unknown species.

He took off leather work gloves and half stuffed them in the front pocket of his jeans. He walked toward her, with a slight limp, smiling, looking like Harry, but more mature, with more defined features. His smile was just as charming, with a little spark of mischief.

She'd had enough of charming to last her a lifetime. Charming wasn't loyal. Charming ran off with another woman. Instead of tears, she unearthed a healthy dose of anger that made the betrayal easier to deal with.

"Can I help you?" He stopped just feet away.

"I'm here to see Etta Forester."

"Etta isn't here." His eyes narrowed, drawing in his nearly blond brows.

"She isn't?" That hadn't been one of the scenarios she'd played through her mind during the two-day drive to Oklahoma. She glanced around, at the green lawn, the big house, the fields behind the house. "She has to be here."

Rejection had been a scenario she'd worked through, and she'd even felt angry when the image of the woman she had never met told Alyson she wasn't welcome here. She had worked through indifference, in case that was the reaction. She had even played through a scene in her mind in which she was welcomed with open arms.

But Etta not being here—that wasn't something she had planned on.

"She's in Florida. She's always in Florida until the end of June." He looked at his watch. "She'll be home in about four weeks."

He knew more than Alyson did. And she still didn't know his name. But then again, he didn't know hers. And he didn't know that her heart had an empty space, and her hands wouldn't cooperate on the piano keys. He didn't know that her father had been raised in this house.

But maybe he did know that. He didn't know that she might have been raised here, had things been different. Whatever *different* meant.

She thought he probably knew that her father was dead. A man she'd never met, the loss tightened in her throat, aching in her heart, hurting worse than losing Dan.

"Are you okay?" He took a step closer, watching her with brown eyes that were deep and earthy. He continued to stare. She was so tired of being the center of attention, the elephant in the room.

She was that dust collector that got put on a

shelf, the odd thing that everyone talked about, wondered where it had come from and why it was there. Sometimes they wondered how it worked. If it quit working, they wondered about that, too.

She was obviously broken. Or maybe cracked. Who would ever know if she was cracked, since they'd never thought she was normal to begin with?

He had asked if she was okay. What did she tell a stranger? How much did she tell? She'd always kept conversations to a minimum—it saved a lot of explanation. She smiled, "I'm fine, just unsure."

"Unsure?"

The unsure part had fallen into the "too much" category. She was a social moron, inept, unable to carry on a conversation without spacing out, going in odd directions that caused her mother to give her "the look."

If she'd thought that being in Oklahoma would suddenly make her normal, she'd been way off. Being here, in middle America, didn't make her the person who suddenly fit in.

"Well?" He continued to watch her, so she smiled, as if everything were okay. And it wasn't. Her legs were trembling and she didn't know what to do with the rest of her life.

She was twenty-eight and a has-been.

"Where do I go from here? I mean, I really didn't think about her not being here. I planned on staying with her."

"And you didn't call?"

No, she hadn't called. She hadn't wanted a rejection on the telephone. She had wanted to escape. If it couldn't be here, it would be somewhere else.

No matter what, she was going to find a place where she could discover who she was. Not knowing about this part of her past, she had thought this would be the best place to start fitting the puzzle of her life together.

"No, I didn't call. It was going to be a surprise."

He liked surprises. Jason Bradshaw started to tell her that, and that he also knew how to listen if she wanted to talk. She looked like a woman who needed someone to talk to. She also looked a lot like Andie Forester. But Andie was wild, a little out of control and somewhere in Colorado running that crazy horse of hers around barrels.

This woman was dressed in a shell-pink cashmere sweater, dove-gray pants, and shoes so pointed he wondered how she got her toes shoved into them. She looked hot, not fashionably *hot,* but *sweltering in the Oklahoma heat* kind of hot. And she looked pretty unhappy.

Beautiful but unhappy, with pale ivory skin, clear-blue eyes and feathery blond hair that hung to her shoulders. Back in the day, he had flirted with women like her and they would either smile and give him a look that invited more flirting, or they gave him the look she'd just given him. It was the "rolled up newspaper on the nose" look, meant to send him back to a corner or under the table.

Not much had sent him running back then. He'd dated, never thinking about the future, settling down or maybe even having a family. He'd thought about riding the next bull, dating the next woman, getting to the next event.

Until God reined him in.

"I'm sure Etta would have liked the surprise." Jason finally came up with something to say. The woman standing in front of him looked about to wilt. Had she told him her name? "Do you want a glass of ice water? I have the key."

He pulled the key to the house out of his pocket and held it up. She glanced at it, and then at the front door, and something lit up in her eyes, something like hopefulness. He wasn't sure what to do with her.

"Who'd you say you're here to see?"

She shot him a look and he knew that had been the wrong question.

Something that sounded like Beethoven rang from inside her purse. He looked at the pink leather bag that probably cost more than most people spent on groceries in a week and waited for her to answer. She stared at him, like she didn't hear it. But she did. He saw the quick flick of those blue eyes, down to the purse and then back to his face.

Her brows shot up in a look that asked "What?"

"You going to answer that?"

She shook her head. He had to think hard to put their conversation back together. People should start calling him Humpty Dumpty. He was the bull rider who'd fallen on his head, and all of the surgeons had tried to put him back together again.

"Fine. So you planned on staying with Etta?" He walked up the stairs of the front porch, right leg first because his left ached from pushing the mower. She came up behind him, smelling as soft and sweet as the sweater she was wearing.

And he had thought he'd left his girl-chasing days behind. This was his new life, detoured from bull riding, and looking for the adult

Jason. When he stopped having headaches from the concussion, he'd get on with that adult thing. As soon as he could remember any thought for more than five minutes.

"I had planned on staying here. If she…" She sighed, her chest heaving and she looked away, her gaze wandering down the country road.

"I see." He pushed the door open and motioned her inside the shadowy interior of the house. It was cool inside, even without the air conditioner turned on, and it smelled as if Etta had been home that morning, slicing cantaloupe and baking muffins.

As they walked, he noticed that she slowed to look into each room. What if she was some kind of classy cat burglar? What if she was casing the joint? Maybe he should call Andie and tell her to come home, or have her contact someone to stay in the house for a few days.

"What's your name?" she asked as they walked down the long hallway to the kitchen at the back of the house. She paused to look at pictures on the wall.

She was taking too much interest in the pictures to be a mere cat burglar. He waited for her to finish. "I'm Jason Bradshaw. I live about a mile down the road. And that's a picture of Etta's son and daughter."

"Son and daughter?"

"Alana is in Florida. James passed away a few years ago."

"I see." Her word was quiet, barely a whisper. She blinked a few times and shook her head. "The water?"

"Are you okay?" He started to reach for her arm, but didn't. She nodded.

"I'm fine." Soft voice, and blue eyes that shimmered. He didn't push for more. He remembered what it was like, to fight that hard to show people he was fine.

He knew what it was, to smile when smiling was the last thing he wanted to do, or felt like doing. He knew how it was to put on an act for so many years that the act became his life.

"In here." He flipped on the light and walked to the fridge. "So, what's your name?"

"Alyson." She looked away, pale and surreal in this country kitchen with the crocheted dishrags, needlepoint verses hanging framed on the walls and the oak, butcher-block table.

"Well, Alyson, here's your water." He handed her a glass of ice water and she took it, sipping and looking away from him. Her hands shook and she looked even paler than she had in the yard. "Why don't you sit down?"

"Thank you." She didn't immediately go to

the table. Instead, she stopped at a needlepoint verse, touching it, reading the Bible verse. "Do you know if she did this?"

"Etta?"

She nodded.

He pointed to the initials in the corner. "I think her granddaughter Andie did that for her."

"Andie?" She turned, setting the water down on the table, droplets splashing over the side.

"She's James's daughter. Etta raised her because James worked away from home."

Alyson, with no last name, sat down. She moved the glass and held it between hands that trembled. Jason sat down across from her, trying to think of something that would make her laugh, or smile. He couldn't handle tears.

But he didn't know her, didn't know how to make her laugh.

"You look like Andie." More than looked like her. He thought maybe that was a piece of the puzzle that he was starting to put together.

"How old is she?"

He had to think about that. "A few years younger than me. Maybe twenty-seven or twenty-eight. She's on the rodeo circuit. She's a barrel racer."

"So no one is here." She lifted the glass again.

"I'm here." He winked.

"I'm afraid you don't count. Sorry." She said it with a smile that lifted shadows from her eyes. Aha, a sense of humor. She might be related to Andie after all.

"What were you wanting with Etta?"

She didn't answer right away. She looked out the window, out gingham curtains that had been closed long enough to let dust coat them. The housekeeper only came in once a month. Alyson, with a well-manicured hand, nails painted the same light shade as her sweater, pulled the curtains back to peer outside.

"I wanted to meet her." She bit into her bottom lip and he wondered if she would cry. She didn't. "I'm…"

He waited.

She turned to face him, smiling a little. "I'm her granddaughter, too."

And that's how she knocked the floor out from under him.

"Stop staring." Alyson slapped the palm of her hand on the table to get the attention of the handsome cowboy sitting across from her. She was still a little shocked, she didn't need his overreaction to her announcement.

She had a sister.

She hadn't found that information in the box

inside her mother's desk when she'd been digging for her bank book.

A sister. That was the missing piece of her life, that part of her she had never been able to connect with. Andie. A memory, fuzzy, faded, but always in the back of her mind. She had thought it was her imagination, not a real memory.

She was still trying to figure out why she'd told the man sitting across from her that she was Etta Forester's granddaughter. Was she that needy? Or was it just easier to share with this man she didn't know?

She had other secrets, but those were hers, locked away where no one could use them against her.

"Okay, no longer staring." He looked out the window, avoiding eye contact. She smiled, because he was trying to make this easy. It was anything but.

She wanted to find a life, a family, and instead she'd found more secrets than she knew how to process. She had enough to deal with. This was supposed to be easy, a place to hide, to get control of her life.

"What am I going to do?"

He looked up. "Can I make a suggestion?"

"Please."

"We can call Etta. She always has solutions to problems. I do think that if you're her granddaughter, she'd want you to stay."

"Okay. We can call her." It wasn't the homecoming she'd planned, but it seemed like the only option. She'd brought money with her, but not enough to rent a house, stay in a hotel, whatever might happen if Etta Forester couldn't be reached. Or worse, didn't want her.

He stood and walked to an old rotary-dial phone on the wall. He lifted a piece of paper, found a number, squinted and dialed. Each time the round rotary dial swished back into place, she cringed. This was it, time to learn the truth, the depth of her mother's lies.

"I'm going to wait in the other room." She pushed herself up from the chair. "I don't think I want to listen to you talk about me."

He nodded, but didn't respond. Alyson walked out of the room, walking into what must have been the parlor. A love seat sat in front of a fireplace and a baby grand piano was in the corner of the room, dust covered, ancient, but beautiful.

Alyson touched the keys and her fingers trembled. She sat down and waited for the fear that always came. But it didn't, not this time, not here. She played softly, for herself, for no one else, the way she had played as a child.

She closed her eyes and tried to bring back a memory, one from childhood, of a piano, a woman with a big smile. Had it been this piano, this house? Had that woman been her grandmother?

It was easy to play this piano, without pressure. Here, in this parlor, she wasn't the golden one. She was no one.

"Beautiful. I've never heard it played like that. Andie tried, but she had absolutely no talent for anything other than riding horses and getting into trouble."

She moved her hands from the keys and turned to face the man who stood in the doorway. He moved his hand, bracing it against the doorframe.

"It's a beautiful piano."

"Your grandmother is on a cruise. Alana is going to try and get hold of her. She's sure her mother will be here as soon as she hears. Alana says she'll try to come as well."

"Okay, that's that. Is there a hotel somewhere?"

"Not in Dawson. But I'm sure your grandmother would want you to stay here. Alana said the same thing—that you should stay."

"I don't know her." She ran her fingers over the keys one last time and walked out from behind the piano. "They don't know me, or if I'm even who I say or think I am."

"I'm pretty sure we all know who you are."

At least they knew. She wondered how that was possible, since she didn't even know who she was. She had always been Alyson Anderson, the pianist. That was the box she fit in. It was her sole identity. Now she wanted more.

Now she had a birth certificate that gave her real name: Alyson Forester. And she had paperwork from the adoption that took place when her mother married Gary. She had her father's signature, signing away his parental rights. As if she were a possession, something to be passed off to another person.

Why had he done that?

"Alana asked me to take you to town to get groceries."

Groceries. Well, that posed a problem. "Isn't there a restaurant?"

"The Mad Cow."

The Mad Cow. She'd learn to cook if that was her only option. But looking at the man in front of her, perspiration-stained and rugged, she thought driving herself would be the best idea.

"I think I'll be fine." She said it with a smile and walked him to the door. He drove away after promising to be back tomorrow to check on her.

Then she was alone in a house where she thought she might have memories. A house where she might learn clues about herself. And her sister, Andie. Her twin? She wasn't sure, but couldn't wait to find out....

Chapter Two

"Jas, where are you going?"

Jason didn't turn the key in the ignition of his truck. Instead, he waited for his sister to hurry across the drive, coming from the direction of the barn where she'd been doctoring a sick mare.

He only knew that because he'd just talked to his dad. At least he remembered one conversation that took place five minutes ago. That showed an improvement. He'd take anything at this point.

"I'm running into town." He tried to think of something funny, something that would wipe the concern from her eyes. He was used to making her laugh. Beth with her short, no-nonsense brown hair, serious brown eyes and a smile that wiped all that seriousness away.

When she smiled. Which wasn't that often.

"Could you get antibiotics for the mare? I called the feed store. They have some in stock." She pulled a tablet out of her pocket and scribbled a note. "Stick that to your nose so you don't forget."

He took the note and nodded. "Will do, Fancy."

"Don't call me that." She socked his arm.

"We've always called…"

She shook her head. "Not since I was ten. Okay?"

"Okay, *Beth*."

"Thanks." She jumped up on the running board of the truck and kissed his cheek. "Where were you going, anyway?"

He glanced down at the paper on the seat next to him. "Grocery store and I'm going to check on Etta's house, feed her horses. I think I need to mow." He sighed. "I think there's something else, but I don't know."

"Me, neither. But it'll come to you." She squinted. "Weren't you mowing at Etta's two days ago? Are you graining her horses? With all the grass they've got?"

"I mowed already?" Of course he had. "I wish I could tell you what I need to do there, Sis, but I can't. I just know that I have to run by her place."

He was suddenly five. Man, he hated this. He'd never had a temper, never wanted to be the guy hitting walls when a ride didn't go well, when the bull won and he lost.

He'd always been the one keeping the family together, making them smile when they wanted to cry. He was the guy who had found faith and shrugged off his old ways.

At least God's memory wasn't lacking the short-term program. Even if it did occasionally feel as if He'd forgotten Jason.

"It'll get better." Beth's hand was on his arm. She was six years younger than him, and she should have been loved by someone who would cherish her.

"Yeah, it'll get better. I have my name and number pinned to my shirt in case I get lost. I'll see you later."

She laughed a little, but he knew she wasn't sure if she should. He grinned and winked, "Laugh, Beth, that was funny."

"Okay, yeah, funny."

"Don't forget to pray for me."

"Right, now I know you've lost it." She walked away and he finally started the truck and headed down the drive.

Toward Etta's. He rubbed the back of his head, still feeling the place where one month ago staples had held his scalp together. He had his long-term memory. Etta wasn't a blur or a memory he had to dig up. He laughed a little, because who could ever forget Etta? But the reason for driving to her house, that one was lost somewhere in his scrambled brain.

Scrambled. He didn't remember the ride that had put him in the hospital. He barely remembered his stay there and then rehab where he'd learned the coping techniques he was still using.

One month and he still couldn't get from point A to point B without a note to tell him why he was going. He could leave the living room and walk into the kitchen, and in the one minute that took, he would forget what he needed. He'd had to move back in with his dad and sister because he couldn't remember to turn off the stove, or that he'd put something in the oven.

He was thirty-one years old and he didn't know how to get his life back. He gripped the steering wheel a little tighter because it felt good to have that control back—at least that.

At least he could drive. He could still ride a horse. He could work cattle. It might hurt a little, but he could cowboy through the pain.

He still had his life. His career, not so much. But maybe it was time to make some decisions about the future. He had a ranch that he hadn't spent nearly enough time on. Maybe it was about time to raise cattle and settle down.

The drive through Dawson didn't take five minutes. There was the one stop sign at the intersection of Main Street and the highway that led to Tulsa. A half-dozen cars were parked in front of the Mad Cow Café and the feed store was busy the way it usually was when the men around town took a break to get out of the afternoon heat. They'd spend the afternoon sitting at the feed store, drinking Coke out of a bottle and telling stories about each other.

He turned and drove down the side road to Etta's. What he'd known before the accident wasn't lost. He knew that Etta was out of town. So why was a car parked in the drive? Why was the front door open?

He parked next to the house and sat there for a minute, staring at the back end of an Audi convertible with Massachusetts plates. Time to think back, to try to retrieve the memory. He pulled his notebook out to see if he'd written himself a note, something to tell him why he would feel the need to check on Etta's house. Nothing.

An alarm sounded, and it had nothing to do with memories, or lost moments. He threw the door open and jumped out of the truck. As he ran up the front walk, windows went up in the living room. The alarm continued to squawk.

He opened the door and the woman in the hallway turned. She glared at him and ran on, into the parlor. She pushed at the bottom of the window.

"Those won't open." He leaned against the doorway, watching her, knowing her, but not. The stench of something burnt clung to the humid air.

She turned, her hair in her face, her cheeks pink. Blue eyes flashed shards of anger, like shattered glass.

"Why won't they open?"

She grabbed a magazine and fanned her face.

"Painted closed. The glass is old and thin. Opening them might break it, so Etta painted the windows closed. Do you have the kitchen windows open?"

"Yes, and the window in the screen door."

He flipped a switch on the wall and an instant rush of air swept through the house. The woman in the pink T-shirt and white Bermuda shorts shot him another look and then she tossed the magazine back on the table.

"What's that?" She walked into the hall and looked up, squinting at the louvered opening.

"Attic fan." He thought *he* was clueless. "It'll

have this cleared out in a minute." He sniffed. "What is that lovely aroma?"

"My lunch."

"Smells, um, appetizing." He followed her down the hall. "What are you doing in Etta's house?"

She stopped, stood frozen for a minute and then turned.

"Excuse me?" She shook her head a little. "You're the one who let me in."

He had let her in? Well, at least he remembered that he had unfinished business here, even if he didn't remember what it was. That was an improvement. "I let you in?"

"Yes, you let me in. You called Alana and then told me it was okay if I stayed here."

"That's good." He could honestly hide his own Easter eggs and not find them.

She made a little growl and walked into the kitchen. When she opened the door to the oven, black smoke rolled out. She sputtered, coughed and grabbed a towel to put over her face.

"I think you're not going to be eating that." He opened the drawer where Etta kept oven mitts and pulled the smoldering box out of the oven.

"No kidding." She pointed to the sink and he tossed it in with dirty dishes and a half-eaten bagel.

"You know you're supposed to take it out of the box, right?" He turned off the water she had turned on to put out the still smoldering pizza.

"But the frozen dinners that I bought go in the oven, box and all. She doesn't have a microwave."

Jason cleared his throat and focused on the window over the sink. He had a feeling that laughter might provoke some kind of really bad reaction from the woman standing in front of him.

"Yeah, so, pizza has to be taken out of the box." He explained. "It can go on the rack or on a baking sheet, but it definitely has to be taken out of the box. And the plastic wrap has to be removed."

"Great. Okay, you've had your laugh, you can go now."

"Look, don't be mad. You have to admit, it is kind of funny." He winked, hoping he still had a little charm left.

She smiled and then she laughed, not a lot, but enough for him to see that she looked a lot like Etta's granddaughter, Andie.

"Yeah, okay, it's a little funny. But…"

"But now you're hungry." He opened the freezer and pulled out another frozen pizza.

"We can try it again. I'll help, if you'll tell me who you are."

"You really don't know?"

"I really don't know." And he no longer felt like laughing. Even the class clown had his moments.

Alyson watched the cowboy standing in her grandmother's kitchen. Maybe he wasn't a cowboy, but he looked like one, in faded jeans, cowboy hat and boots. He unwrapped the frozen pizza, opened the oven door and slid the pizza onto the wire rack.

He turned around and she didn't know what to do now, because he didn't seem to know her and she couldn't forget him. Last night as she wandered through this big house, discovering her family for the first time, she'd thought of him.

She'd thought of him all day yesterday, when she'd been alone in this big house, not knowing anyone, and not really knowing herself. Two days ago she'd found out she had a sister. She was still reeling from the depths of her mother's deception.

"You were going to tell me your name." He leaned against the counter, arms crossed over his chest, the cowboy hat on his head cocked a little to the side.

"Alyson Anderson. I'm Etta's granddaughter."

"You're Etta's granddaughter?"

"I am." And she had a sister who looked so much like her, it ached in her heart to know that she'd missed out knowing her all these years, and she didn't know why they'd been separated.

Instead of the answers she thought she'd find here, she had more questions.

Last night she had looked at photo albums of a family she couldn't remember, a family she had been taken from. She had cried because the father who had held her in those pictures, pictures taken when she was a toddler, was gone. And she had been denied the opportunity to ever know him.

"Alyson, Etta's granddaughter." He nodded, still leaning against the counter. "And Andie must be your sister."

"I'm assuming that's the case."

"Assuming? You don't know?"

She shook her head and turned away from him, concentrating on the pitcher of tea she'd made that morning, pretending she stood in country kitchens every day, pouring iced tea into glasses shaped like kegs with wooden handles. The mugs were the most normal thing she'd found in the kitchen.

Her grandmother was a little different. Or so she'd decided in her exploration of the quaint Victorian. Her grandmother had shelves of books. She had Bibles and she had books on living off the land in the sixties. There were pictures of a commune in one photo album. She'd found a spinning wheel upstairs and wool. She was wearing a pair of socks she'd found in a basket next to the spinning wheel. Itchy wool socks, but they were somehow comforting.

And too hot for late May. But she didn't care.

"What are you doing here?" He opened the oven door and peeked in at the pizza. "Almost done."

"I'm here to see my grandmother."

"Right."

He said it in a way that implied he didn't believe her. And she guessed he was right. She wanted to meet her grandmother, but she had more reasons for showing up in Dawson, Oklahoma.

She was running away. Did twenty-eight-year-old women run away? Did they pack up without telling anyone where they were going and take off without saying goodbye? Did they ignore the phone when it rang, refusing to talk to family? Her younger sister had done something similar, but Laura had taken something important with her.

Laura had taken Dan.

That was hard to forget. She could work on the forgiving part. That was the consensus—she needed to forgive. People said it as if she should be able to sweep the vastness of her pain under a rug, along with the dust she'd shaken out of her mother's box of secrets.

That was something no one knew—that she'd found that box. They assumed that all of her pain had to do with Laura and Dan. But that box had pushed her to finally leave. She had packed up her clothes, left the key to her apartment with the doorman and walked away.

Jason rummaged through the cabinets, pulling out a baking sheet and a spatula. She watched as he opened the oven and slid out the rack. It seemed easy for him, sliding the baking sheet under the pizza and pulling it out. Of course she could have done it.

She would do it next time. And next time she wouldn't burn the house down.

"Do you want me to cut this?" He opened a drawer and pulled out a knife.

"Might as well. Why didn't you remember me?" Should she be afraid of him? But her grandmother seemed to trust him. He was mowing her lawn and he had a key to the house.

He had probably known her grandmother his entire life.

He pushed the knife into the pizza and glanced up at her, smiling. "I had an accident."

She nodded and watched as he worked the knife through the pizza, not as easily as he should have, or as easily as she would have imagined. She thought about offering to help, but she didn't because he seemed to be the type of man who always wanted to be strong.

"What kind of accident?" She took a step, putting herself next to him.

"A bull." He gave her a sideways look and went back to work on the pizza. "I'm a bull rider."

"I see. Wouldn't it be better to ride a horse?"

He laughed and turned, pushing up the cowboy hat that had kept her from getting a good look at him, at his brown eyes. He had eyes that were a mix of laughter and pain. He had stories.

She wanted his stories, not her own.

"You don't know what bull riding is?" He grabbed a paper plate off the holder on the counter and handed it to her. "Eat your pizza."

"I know what it is." She shrugged, hoping to

look smart, like she really did know what the sport entailed. She'd seen pictures. She had seen it on TV.

She slid pizza onto the plate and handed it to him. "Are you going to eat?"

"No." But he took the plate. "Sure, why not."

She followed him to the table. "So, what happened when you were riding the bull?"

"I got stepped on." He sat down across from her. His hand went to the back of his head. "Let's pray."

He took off his hat and sat it on the chair next to him.

"Pray?" She looked at the hand he'd reached out for hers. She met the intent gaze, brown eyes with flecks of green.

"Bless our food." His hand grasped hers and he bowed his head. And she stared, not meaning to stare. She'd met so many people in her life. She'd never met the type of man that held her hand and bowed his head to pray over frozen pizza.

Until today.

His head was bowed. She followed, bowing hers. His strong, warm hands held her hands and soft words thanked God for their food. For frozen pizza. At his "Amen," she pulled her hands back.

"The bull stepped on you." Back to something easy to talk about. For her.

It probably wasn't easy for him.

"The bull. Yes. I was unconscious for…" He looked up and then shook his head. "Sorry, I can't find it."

"It?"

He looked at her. "I lose words. It's like having a bucket with a hole in it. I keep trying to fill it up, but it keeps leaking out. Twelve hours. I was out for twelve hours."

"I'm sorry."

He shrugged. "No need. I'm alive. It upset my plans a little, but, since I can't remember most of them, I'll survive."

His smile said it was a joke, as if it didn't matter. But it had to matter.

"Aren't you angry?"

Her plans had fallen apart in April. Her wedding would have been two weeks ago. She should have been in Europe on her honeymoon.

She had a note with the scrawled handwriting of her sister, begging forgiveness. Alyson looked at it every day, trying to figure out why she'd been tossed aside, and how her sister could have done this to her.

Dan had called to tell her that Laura knew how to enjoy life. As if Alyson didn't. It wasn't about not knowing how, it was about never getting the chance.

"No, I'm not angry." He reached for his hat, but he didn't put it back on. "That isn't true. Sometimes I am mad. Isn't that what happens when things don't go the way we expected?"

Alyson had never thought of herself as an angry person. Lately she'd been angry. Or maybe bitter. She stood, picking up the paper plate and empty mug.

"Will your memory improve?" She tossed the paper plates in the trash and opened the door of the dishwasher to stick the forks in the basket.

"It's getting better. They don't have answers about how far I'll progress, when or how. Physical therapy helped the physical problems, or is helping, but the other..." He shrugged.

"When did this happen?"

"Five weeks."

"April?"

He nodded.

April had been a bad month. April Fool. That was what she'd called herself when she got the note. She walked to the door and looked out, at the backyard, at the barn and the fields. She turned back to face him and he was watching her.

"There are horses in the field," she said, but of course he knew that.

"Yeah, the horses. I'm here to check them." He pulled a small notebook out of his pocket. "And your name is…"

She smiled this time because he glanced up at her, a little lost, unsure. "Alyson Anderson."

He wrote it down in his notebook and whispered it a few times. "I won't forget."

She was forgettable, so she thought he might.

Jason walked down the hall and flipped off the attic fan. The rush of air through the house stilled immediately. He glanced into the sitting room where Etta spent most of her time, usually knitting or quilting, and sometimes painting. Photo albums were scattered across the sofa.

The woman next to him turned a little pink. "I found them."

"I'm sure it's okay if you look at them." He rubbed his cheek, feeling the raspy growth of whiskers he'd forgotten to shave that morning.

"I don't know the people in those pictures." She didn't look at him.

"How did that happen?"

She shrugged. "I'm not really sure. I'm still trying to put it all together, why they're here, and I'm not."

"I can look at the album with you, if you like." Sit next to her on the sofa, with her soft, floral scent floating around him, reminding him of something, someone.

He nearly laughed, because he was sure that the memory was of her. It was her perfume that brought it back.

"The horses," she reminded him.

"You can help me feed. I'll help you with the pictures."

She nodded and he followed her to the sofa. She picked up the three albums and stacked them on the coffee table. When he sat down next to her, she picked up the first one and opened it to a page with Andie's baby pictures.

"Is this Andie?" She touched a picture of a toddler and her hands trembled, so did her voice.

"I think." He glanced at her. "Or it could be you."

She ignored the comment that pointed out the obvious.

"What's she like?"

It was a little ironic that he had no short-term memory, and the woman sitting next to him knew nothing about her life. Or at least about her family.

He flipped through the album and found several pages of Andie at different rodeo events.

"She's wild." He grinned, drawing up memories of a girl who had outrun the cops and hid her truck in his barn. "She's a little rebellious."

"What does she like to do?" Alyson pulled out a picture of Andie on her barrel horse. "Other than rodeos."

"That's about it. She fishes and hunts. I've seen her ride a bull. She's a little crazy."

She'd broken hearts all over the county. Not his.

He'd steered clear of Etta's granddaughter. If he were in his right mind, he'd steer clear of the one sitting next to him.

She put her hand on the page and stopped him from turning. Her finger dropped on the photo of James Forester, Andie's dad.

"Who is that?"

"I think that must be James. It's an older picture, probably before you were born. And the woman next to him is Alana, your aunt."

"Oh." She looked out the window and he didn't know what to do. She was a stranger. She had stiff shoulders and her chin was up, like she was holding it together as best as she could. He didn't know how to make her smile. He didn't know her well enough to make her laugh.

He definitely didn't know her well enough to put his arms around her and tell her that she could cry if she needed to cry. As he waited, her hand went up, flicking at her cheek, at tears he couldn't see.

"I'm not sure why I'm here," she whispered, still looking away from him, out the window. He wasn't sure if the words were for him. She turned and smiled. "I'm sorry, you didn't come here for this."

Jason stood, not sure, really not sure. He hadn't had a lot of experience with that feeling, not until last month. Lately it seemed as if his whole life was about being unsure.

In this case, he took a step back, knowing it was better to leave well enough alone. He'd always heard that saying. He could honestly say that this was the first time in his life that he really got what it meant.

He'd rather face a charging bull than this woman and her well of emotions.

"I'll go on out and feed the horses. If you need anything…"

"Thank you." She turned and there were tears sliding down her cheeks. What should he say? She'd found her family, and lost a dad, all in a span of a twenty-four hours.

"I'm sorry."

She nodded. And he left her there alone, sitting on Etta's satin sofa, the photo album in her lap.

Chapter Three

Alyson didn't want to need a cowboy. She didn't want to need anyone. Not now, when she was determined to find out who she was without her family planning her life, without a publicist or the media telling her who they thought she was. She was twenty-eight. She was going to figure out what she liked, what she wanted.

She would find out what it meant to be Alyson Forester, from Dawson, Oklahoma and not Alyson Anderson, child prodigy.

She didn't want to need anyone, but she also didn't want to be alone, not with her heart aching and her throat still constricted tight and painful with grief over losing a father she'd never had the chance to know.

But if she closed her eyes and breathed deep

in this house, was it his scent that she remembered? Did she remember a moment when her father had held her tight and told her he loved her and he was sorry? It was a vague memory, or maybe wishful thinking.

Being here made it all real, unlike at home when she'd searched for his name on the Internet, tracing him here through articles about his rodeo life, and his death in a car accident.

He'd been a stranger she'd read about. Now, being here, he was real. Her memories, fuzzy and unfocused, were becoming clear.

And she had a sister, a sister who was probably more like their father. Andie had spirit. She looked like someone who knew how to fight for what she wanted. Alyson wondered if there was any of that within her, that fighting spirit that grabbed at life, at dreams.

Of course she had that in her. She was here. She had finally walked away from her life. She had contacted the lawyer friend who had helped her for the last ten years, secretly guiding her in how to keep her money safe, how to keep her schedule her own. He had encouraged her, and told her it was time to go.

And she'd walked away, taking her clothes and her only other rebellion, the iPod downloaded with Martina McBride and Miranda

Lambert songs. Now that she thought about it, it was funny how she'd always loved country music. Maybe that had been a clue about her life, and who she really was.

She walked to the back door of her grandmother's house. On the wall was another needlepoint verse. This one said: Trust in the Lord with all your heart and lean not unto your own understanding.

Trust in a God she had never really understood. He was a cathedral, aging artwork in museums and a name people muttered when they were angry.

Her grandmother trusted. Obviously trusted.

Alyson didn't know how to trust a God she didn't know. Not when she barely knew herself.

Four days ago she had left Boston. She wasn't going to call it running away, like the message her mother had left on her phone, that she had run away and she had responsibilities. Children ran away—not grown women.

Alyson wouldn't let them call this running away, or a breakdown. This was finding herself. She was doing what she wanted to do, maybe for the first time in her life.

She had a feeling that twenty-five years ago she had wanted to stay here.

Outside was a world she knew so little about.

It was hard to know real life when her childhood, her teen years, had been spent with a piano, or on a stage. She'd always lived in a bubble.

She hadn't even wanted to marry Dan. He had just seemed like the right choice. He had been the next step. He was a composer. He loved music. He loved to travel.

He loved her sister.

It wasn't a broken heart that ached inside her when she thought of that. It was something deeper. It was betrayal.

It might be bitterness.

If she stayed in Dawson, she could buy a little house on a quiet corner, get some cats and be the crazy cat lady people in town talked about fifty years from now. She could bake cookies for neighbor children who were afraid to come in her yard, and talk to herself at the store.

She'd give everyone something to talk about.

Crazy people probably didn't plan going crazy. So maybe she was still sane.

Through the window on the back door she watched the barn and saw the cowboy, Jason, as he walked out of a shed and across the lawn to a corral. She had walked out there that morning, taking her cup of coffee to watch as wispy fog covered the valley and horses grazed, tails switching at flies. The sun had touched it all with a golden hue. It had been something, to sit on a bench in the yard and watch the sun rise and the fog dissipate.

She pushed the door open now and walked out, knowing it was a mistake, to go out there, to follow that man around the barn, wanting to be around him, around someone.

As she walked across the lawn a dog joined her. He was tall, leggy and had wiry black hair. She stepped back, unsure. The animal wagged its tail and she took a few careful steps. It followed.

Her chest did a familiar squeeze, a painful clench that didn't belong here, not in Oklahoma in this peaceful setting. She closed her eyes and took a deep breath. When she opened them, the dog was still there. Her breath still felt caught in her lungs.

"Okay, dog, I'm not sure if you're friendly or not, so back off. Go on."

A whistle called the dog away from her. She turned toward the barn and he was there, standing in the opening. He was a little bow-legged, in the cowboy way, and it was appealing, cute. He held a hand out to the dog, sliding fingers through the hair at the back of the animal's neck.

He was Robert Redford rugged, standing in the doorway of a barn, petting a dog, but smiling at her. And she had never experienced life like this.

"That's a look." The cowboy with the Oklahoma drawl spoke when she got closer. "The dog isn't mean."

"Is he yours?" Could he be Etta's dog?

"He doesn't belong to anyone, but everyone feeds him. They toss him scraps at the Mad Cow. The convenience store gives him leftovers. Everyone in town looks out for Mutt."

"Why?"

His head tilted to one side. "Because he doesn't have anyone. He got dumped a year or so ago. People started feeding him and the vet gives him medical care, keeps him updated on his shots. He's just a good dog and he's refused to stay at any one house."

"Oh. So I can feed him?"

"You can. I'm sure Etta does."

She reached to pet the dog and its tail wagged hard enough to shake its back end. "Can I help with the horses? I can feed them so you don't have to drive over here."

"Come on, I'll show you what to do." He glanced back. "It's probably a good idea. You never know when I'll forget."

She followed him back into the barn. She had been in stables, but this barn was different. It was old. It was tall, with a hayloft in the top. Dust swirled in the light that shined through the front door. It smelled of animals, hay and the past.

The dog ran around the barn, sniffing in empty stalls and then barking a shrill bark when he found something. Alyson glanced at Jason and he shrugged.

"Probably a mouse or a cat." He walked into the corner stall where the dog had something cornered. "Kitten."

Alyson peeked inside as Jason picked up the yellow tabby by the scruff of the neck. The kitten yowled and hissed, spitting and angry. Alyson reached for it and it slashed little claws at her hand.

"Did it get you?" Jason kept hold of the spitting little feline.

"No. What do we do with it?"

"Grab a towel out of the feed room and we'll wrap him up and see if we can calm him down."

He nodded toward an open door. She stepped into the feed room and glanced around, finally finding a pile of old towels, folded and shoved in a cabinet. She grabbed a couple and walked back outside. He was still holding the kitten out from him, but it wasn't hissing now, just looking around.

"Won't that hurt it, holding it that way?"

He shook his head. "This is how the momma cat carried him. He probably got a little big for his britches and ran off. He's old enough to be on his own."

He took the towel and wrapped it tight around the kitten.

"Now what?" She touched the kitten's head. Her first step toward being the neighborhood cat lady.

"Take him. Just keep the towel around him so he can't scratch you."

Alyson took the kitten. She'd always loved cats. They were funky and independent. This one struggled a little against her, but the towel around his legs kept him from clawing.

"Should I feed him?"

"Probably a good idea. You'll have to run to town and get cat food. Or if you have bread and eggs. Sometimes my sister tears up bread and beats an egg into it."

"I can do that. I'll get food tomorrow. The lady at the Mad Cow said I should go to Grove for groceries, not to the convenience store."

"She's right. The convenience store doesn't carry much." He slipped a knife out of his pocket and cut the string on a bale of hay he must have tossed down from the hayloft.

"My grandmother just leaves her horses here when she goes to Florida? How long is she gone?"

"A few months. I watch them, or Beth, my sister, does. We ride them when the weather is warm. And they get a lot of attention from neighbor kids."

"What about Andie? Doesn't she live here?"

"She's gone a lot. She barrel races, and she has friends around the country. She's…"

"She's what?"

"She's always been a free spirit."

"I see." She held the kitten close and heard a soft purr. "I think he's calming down."

"Yeah, probably. But if you let him go, he'll be gone." He picked up a few flakes of hay and walked out the back door of the barn. Alyson followed.

The horses were there, waiting. There were three of them, one brown, one a light gold and one with spots on his rump. She liked that one. He had gentle eyes and had nuzzled her hand this morning.

"What kind of horses are they?"

He glanced back at her and then he pointed to the brown horse. "That one with the black mane and tail is a bay, that's her color. She's an Arabian, though. Etta bought her somewhere outside of Tulsa. She saw this horse, half-starved in a round pen and she pulled into the drive of the house and told the people to name their price. Goldie here is a Palomino. She's Andie's old barrel horse. This Appaloosa, with the white rump is the mare that Etta rides."

"They're beautiful. Maybe while I'm here I can ride."

"How long are you staying?" He glanced back at her as he dumped the hay in piles a good distance apart. "Or have you already told me?"

"I don't know how long I'll stay." She hadn't thought about it. How long did it take a woman to find herself? How long would her grandmother want her here, in this house, this town?

What if she didn't want Alyson at all? Maybe there was a reason Alyson's mother had taken her away and left Andie behind.

Jason pulled out his list, marking off feeding Etta's horses. He shoved the notebook back into his pocket and watched as Alyson leaned over the fence, trying to pet the Appaloosa while still holding the yowling kitten. The horse moved a little closer and Alyson scratched its neck.

"I need to take a drive out to the youth camp. Do you want to go along?"

"Youth camp?" She turned from the horse and leaned against the fence.

"Camp Hope. A good friend of mine and her husband run it." He ran a thought through his mind. "You could volunteer if you're here for a while."

She held the kitten tight, like a five-year-old with a new pet. That's what it was about her—she acted as if everything was new. "What could I do there?"

"I don't know, maybe play the piano."

Her eyes widened and she shook her head. "No, I don't play the piano."

He closed his eyes, trying to drag the memory back, surprised that it had been there at all. He remembered. She'd been playing a hymn, probably from one of Etta's songbooks. That's why the memory had stuck with him. He knew the song. It was one his mother had sung, a long time ago.

"I remember you playing."

"You didn't even remember me being here." She walked past him and he caught up with her.

"I remember you playing the piano." He followed her through the barn and across the yard to the house, his walk a kind of skip as he tried to keep up. "I can hear the song you were playing. I think it might have been 'It is Well.'"

"It was." They reached the house and he opened the back door for her. She slid through, still holding the cat.

"So, you'll go with me. You might as well get out and see what's going on in the community. It'll get old, sitting in this house waiting for Etta to get back."

"I won't get bored. I love having nothing to do, nowhere to go. You have no idea."

No, he didn't. "So, tell me, why do you want to be here, with nothing to do?"

She glanced back, over her shoulder, her eyes a little narrowed. She looked like the kitten, about to hiss. He laughed a little, because that was Andie, always ready to strike out at someone or something.

"I lived in Boston." She held the kitten in one arm and opened the fridge door. "I've lived in San Francisco. I've lived in Seattle."

"And now you're here? That's a big change."

"I've never lived here, or not since I was little. I want to know what this place is like. This was my father's world."

He nodded and somehow he retrieved the memory. His head was starting to pound.

"James. He was here when he wasn't on the road."

"Where else did he go?" She turned quick, spilling a little of the milk she had opened to pour in a bowl.

"Not too much milk, it'll make him sick." Jason opened the loaf of bread she must have bought at the convenience store. It was half-stale and had a price tag on it that was twice what she should have paid. He pulled the piece of bread into pieces and dropped them in with the milk. She had cracked an egg to add to the mixture.

"What about my dad, about James Forester?" She opened a drawer and pulled out a fork.

"Years ago he was a saddle bronc rider. Later he drove a truck. He also worked offshore oil rigs. He was gone a lot."

"Who took care of my sister?"

"Etta raised her when James was gone. But he came into town and he lived here when he wasn't working."

Alyson glanced away. He followed her gaze to the frame with a dozen or so family pictures. And not one of them was of her. That was a shame. There was a picture of Etta and Andie dressed up for the Fourth of July celebration a few years back. They'd won first place in that competition. They'd been a pair, always having fun, and fighting.

"Would I like her?" She turned her attention back to him, serious blue eyes locking on him, expecting answers.

He hadn't expected this, to get dragged into what should have been personal. But she was waiting, holding that kitten against her and the bowl in the other hand.

"Etta is a free spirit. Andie is, too. You'll like them both."

Alyson put the bowl of milk and eggs on the floor and sat the kitten on the ground next to it. They stepped back and watched as the ragged little guy hissed and slurped in turn. And then he was gone, running out of the kitchen and down the hall, paws sliding on the polished hardwood floors.

"What now?" Alyson went after the cat.

"You'll never catch him and Etta is going to be ticked. She hates cats."

Alyson turned, her face a little pale. "Now you tell me?"

He grinned. "Head injury, remember?"

"What do I do?"

He shrugged. "You'll catch him and Etta will forgive you."

How could she not forgive her granddaughter?

He shook off the mental wandering that could only lead to trouble. He didn't have enough space in his brain for that kind of trouble. "I have to go."

"To the camp?"

"Yeah, of course." He pulled the notebook out of his pocket. "First to the feed store."

He held the notebook up and the words blurred and then doubled. The ache in the back of his head tripled. He slipped the notebook back into his pocket and blinked a few times to clear his vision.

"Are you okay?" A female voice from too far away. He looked up and she was watching him, her eyes focused and full of concern. He managed a smile.

"Of course I am."

"You look pale." She rummaged through the cabinet and while he tried to get it together, she ran water into the mug and held it out. "Drink this."

He pulled off the hat that suddenly seemed too tight and wiped a hand across his forehead. She pushed the water into his hand and he took it, because she was determined.

"Thanks." He set the cup on the counter.

A cool hand was on his arm, holding him closer than he should have been to her, to someone who smelled like lavender and roses on a summer day.

She led him down the hall to the parlor. He let her, because of lavender and roses, and because he couldn't undo her hand from his arm. And he didn't really want to.

Which meant he wasn't too far gone.

"Sit down."

She backed him up to the wing chair next to the piano. He sat, closing his eyes and leaning his head back to rest, just for a minute.

The screen door slammed and he didn't want to open his eyes. But there were footsteps and perfume that hung over the air like some kind of heavy-duty air freshener. He opened his eyes.

"What in the world is going on here?" Etta Forester stood in the doorway of the parlor, a vision in tie-dyed clothes, lavender hair and a floppy, wide-brimmed hat.

It was a bad time to be seeing double.

The woman standing next to his chair looked like she was about to faint. He barely remembered her name, but he felt a lot like the ten-year-old Jason after he'd gotten caught playing house with Amy Baxter, his next-door neighbor at the time.

This was her grandmother? Alyson had

thought she was coming to a normal, sane world. She thought she had left crazy behind. Maybe the town cat lady wasn't as far-fetched as she thought. A giggle sneaked up on Alyson, surprising her, and she laughed. And then her grandmother laughed.

"Girl, I've wanted to hug you for twenty-something years. Come here." Etta Forester took the few steps that brought them together and then her arms were around Alyson, holding tight.

Etta stepped back. "Well, it don't look like they ruined you too awful bad. A little too much like a spit-polished boot, but you'll do. I'd say you've had your first scuff marks in the last few weeks. Is that what…"

Etta jerked around, and then leaned to look under the sofa. "What in the world. Is that a nasty old cat in my house?"

Another laugh, this one deep, male. Alyson glared at the man sitting in her grandmother's velvet wingback.

"Yes, it is a cat. He told me to bring it in and feed it."

"I didn't tell you to let it go." He struggled to sit up. Alyson held out a hand and he pulled himself to his feet.

And he didn't let go of her hand, not for a

long moment, and it wasn't easy, to untangle herself from the emotion that happened in that moment. The connection between them started in her fingers and slid down her arms, straight to her heart. She couldn't breathe, couldn't move away from his touch.

"Jason Bradshaw, what is the matter with you? Bull get you down?"

"Just a little. Some head—"

Etta waved her hand. "I read about it on the Internet. Concussion and some torn ligaments in your knee. How's your noggin?"

"My noggin hurts and you're pretty lucky that I remember you."

Etta patted his cheek. "Honey, you couldn't forget an old bird like me."

"You *are* unforgettable." Jason rubbed the back of his head and Alyson wondered if he was as okay as he pretended.

"There's that cat again." Etta pointed to the love seat. "Get that thing outta here. My goodness, you're here for what, two days and you're already dragging in strays. You always were animal crazy."

Alyson turned, she held her grandmother's gaze and she couldn't look away. "I was animal crazy?"

"Of course you were. Drove your mother

insane. Well, everything drove that high-maintenance female insane."

"I'm sorry about the kitten. It was hungry." She glanced at Jason. "And it wasn't his fault."

Being around her grandmother seemed to push both of them back in time about twenty years, Alyson realized. They were suddenly children, apologizing and trying to make excuses for their bad behavior.

"The kitten doesn't have to go, but you'll need a litter box and some food for the mangy-looking thing."

"Since Etta is here, I think I can go now." Jason walked to the door. He paused at the opening and leaned against it a little and Alyson remembered he'd done that yesterday. She realized now that it wasn't about being relaxed. He was holding himself up.

"Jason, do you need a ride home?" Etta was more observant. It didn't take her two days to notice when a man wasn't as strong as he pretended to be.

"No, I think I'm fine. I just need a minute to get my legs back under me. Take care of each other. Etta, I'm glad you're home."

"Well, thanks to you I came back early and cut short a perfectly lovely cruise with friends."

"I did that?" Jason shook his head. "I guess I probably did."

"We'll blame it on Alana. She called the ship. I got off at the next port and flew to Tulsa."

"You didn't have to do that." Alyson found it hard to believe that anyone would do that. And as she was taking it all in, Jason was saying goodbye. Her one familiar link in this town, a man who couldn't remember her name.

He left, walking down the sidewalk to his truck, slow, even steps, and still that cowboy swagger. Alyson watched through the gauzy curtains as he got into his truck, pulling himself into the seat and sitting for a minute.

"We should probably drive him," she whispered.

A hand touched her shoulder. Her grandmother stood behind her, staring out the window with her. "He wouldn't thank you for that. A cowboy likes to take care of himself. He's stronger than most. He's been through a lot and came out just fine."

"What's he been through?"

"Now honey, if I told you that, then you wouldn't have the fun of getting to know him. Getting to know a man, that's part of the adventure."

Alyson watched him drive away. "I'm not

here to get to know a man. I'm here to find out who I am."

Her grandmother put an arm around her shoulders. "I'm glad you're home, Alyson girl, glad you're home."

Chapter Four

Alyson stood in the center of her grandmother's parlor and thought about Etta's words. *Glad she was home.* Was this home? Or just a place to hide for a little while, until she figured out her next move, where she went from here?

"Are you going to tell me what happened?" Etta flipped on a light and pulled the drapes open, sending a light cloud of dust across the room.

Alyson sneezed a few times as sunlight poured into the room, the beams catching the particles of dust that had flown from the drapes. Etta didn't seem to be bothered by the sunlight or the dust. She swiped her finger across the windowsill and shook her head before turning back to face Alyson.

"Well?" Alyson's grandmother was a tall, thin woman with hair that wasn't gray, but a shade of lavender. Silver hoops dangled from her ears and her clothes were breezy and tie-dyed, like the ones Alyson had found upstairs in the room with the spinning wheel.

"I needed to find you."

Etta's brows went up and she shook her head. She pointed to the photo albums on the sofa and glanced back at Alyson. And then it hit her, that maybe she shouldn't be here. Maybe she should have run to anyplace but Oklahoma. She knew people in California. She had friends in Chicago. She could have gone anywhere.

And she'd picked Dawson, Oklahoma. She'd picked Etta. She wanted answers to questions that had lingered in the back of her mind for years. There had always been flashes of memory, missing pieces and unanswered questions.

She had tried to research a few years earlier, when she first moved into her own apartment, but she'd hit dead ends. Maybe because she hadn't really known what she was searching for. It was hard to search for something that felt like child-hood dreams—nothing real, nothing tangible.

"You're here because something happened." Etta sat down on the piano bench and ran her fingers over the keys. "You played it when you were a little bitty thing. I knew then, when you were barely talking, that you had a gift."

A gift, or was it a curse? Etta couldn't know the pressure. She couldn't know what it felt like, to never really have a childhood, to always be playing, to always be *on* for the people around her. Her weekends had been spent with her mother, poring over articles written about her performances. Nothing was more fun for an eight-year-old than to read about every wrong note she'd played.

And what happened to the prodigy when she became an adult, with hands that trembled and fear that squeezed the air from her lungs? What did she do when the pills stopped working?

"I didn't know about you, about my family here." Alyson walked to the window, she looked out at the quiet country lane. A truck pulling a trailer loaded with hay lumbered down the road, a Border Collie standing on the bales of hay.

Alyson turned to face her grandmother. "I had memories that I couldn't figure out. I stopped questioning my mother years ago. She wouldn't answer."

"I'm sorry." Etta stood, closing the cover over the keys of the piano and walking up behind Alyson. An arm, comforting and strong, wrapped around Alyson's shoulders and pulled her close. "You and Andie were the victims. I couldn't stop what they did, the way they decided to end things. I just prayed that someday you'd come back."

"I guess your prayers have been answered." The words were empty, because Alyson had never prayed, not real prayers that counted. She'd prayed to go to Europe, to have a pony, and to survive. That had been a prayer that counted. She just hadn't realized it at the time.

"Yes, my prayers have been answered. But it isn't all about having you here. It's about having you happy."

Alyson walked away from the window, away from her grandmother's embrace. She stopped in front of the photo albums she'd left on the coffee table. She'd found pictures of herself in those albums, a toddler who smiled.

How did she tell her grandmother about the pills she took for anxiety, and about falling apart? How did she talk about how it felt to look in the mirror and see a fraud, someone so far from the perfect person everyone thought she was, that she didn't even recognize the person looking back at her?

She picked up the album and opened to pictures of her father and her sister. Andie. She whispered the name and closed her eyes. There were so many missing pieces of her life she wondered how she had ever felt whole.

Had she ever felt whole?

She wasn't sure that she was even there yet, not even with this knowledge, with this family she had missed out on, and with Etta standing next to her.

"He loved you."

Alyson closed her eyes and tried to remember that love, those arms, and how it had felt to be a part of their lives, a part of Etta's home and her family. Vaguely, she vaguely remembered him tossing her into the air and catching her.

There were other memories, memories that made her want to cry. She shook her head to clear the images of driving away. Images that had been explained away as childhood nightmares.

"I wish he would have come after me, after us." Alyson didn't mean to make it an accusation against a man who could no longer defend himself, but it happened.

"Aly, he couldn't. They made a deal. Your mother and father were two different people. James was a country boy. Caroline was city. He grew up in church. Your mother didn't. They couldn't find a middle ground."

"So he let her leave? With me?"

"That was the deal. He took Andie, she got you."

"*Parent Trap* was cute and funny, and it had a happy ending. My parents really did this to their children." As if they were property, as if their feelings hadn't mattered.

"I know." Her grandmother's voice was soft, unlike her image in those tie-dyed clothes.

And now the most difficult question. "How did they decide who kept whom? Why did he keep Andie?"

Etta sighed. "Andie wouldn't have survived your mother."

Alyson shook her head. Did that make her a survivor? Did they honestly see her as the strong one? When she looked at those pictures of Andie, smiling, laughing on the back of a horse, and then she thought of her own child-hood, she didn't get that.

Andie looked stronger than Alyson had ever felt.

"How is Andie?"

"Andie's good. She's a free spirit, going all over the country, from rodeo to rodeo. She's going to love you, though."

The empty space in her heart grew and there didn't seem to be a way to fill it. This could have been her world, her life, and instead she had been her mother's prized possession, but never a daughter—that position had gone to her younger siblings.

Alyson's childhood had been spent performing. She had been paraded on programs, on stages, where they would test her with a song and then she'd play it. She remembered them trying to trick her, to break her with a song she might not know.

She had worn the responsibility of not letting her parents down, not letting her family down.

"We'll work through this, Alyson. I want you here, and you can stay as long as you'd like." Etta smiled big. "Honey, you can stay forever if that's what you want. It's whatever you decide."

Alyson could decide. Of course she could, but she also knew that there were obligations looming that she couldn't avoid. Sooner or later she would have to return to her life.

But for now, Alyson Anderson was Alyson Forester and that required a change.

"Do you think we could go shopping?"

Etta smiled. "Honey, now you're speaking my language."

As they turned to walk out of the room, the kitten shot past them, a ragged little feline with cobwebs on his whiskers.

"I can't believe you brought that animal into my house."

"He's cute, though."

Etta laughed. "Mangy is never cute. Now don't let me forget that we need comfortable shoes if we're going to work at Camp Hope."

The shift in conversation took Alyson by surprise. "When do we do that?"

"Next week." Etta grabbed her purse and keys that she'd dropped on the table just inside the front door. "We'll stop by later and talk to Jenna and Adam."

As they walked out the door, Alyson was thinking of Camp Hope, then her thoughts turned to Jason Bradshaw. She wanted him to remember her, because memories shouldn't be one-sided.

Jason landed wrong when he jumped out of his truck at Camp Hope. Too bad the pills he'd taken for his head weren't going to undo this. He leaned against his truck and flexed his leg, grimacing at the pull in his knee. He had more problems with his body than someone thirty years older than him. Or that's what the doctor had said the last time Jason had kept an appointment.

And with that verdict the doctor had also told him it was about time for him to think about retiring from bull riding. Jason shrugged off the advice, and didn't want to think about it, even now.

He limped away from his truck and started toward the dorm where Clint and Adam were working. Clint was on the ladder. Distracted, Jason didn't see the two boys running toward him until they hit him head on, wrapping six-year-old arms around his waist and nearly knocking him off his feet.

"Whoa, guys, what's up?" He hugged them close and they did what they'd always done, each claimed a leg to hug and he would walk with them holding tight.

"We've missed you." Both boys shouted. This must be what a sugar high looked like.

"I missed you guys, too. But did you maybe have too much candy today?" He stopped, grimacing because they were heavier than when they started this game a few years back. "Do you think you could give an old guy a break and walk with me today?"

They let go of his legs and sat back on the ground, staring up as if he'd lost his mind. "Do we gotta?" David asked.

"Yeah, sorry guys, today we gotta." He held out his hands and the two grabbed, one on each hand. "Where is everybody?"

As in their parents, Jenna and Adam, and their uncle Clint.

"They have to get this place ready for kids." Timmy, always the mimic.

"They're fixing the roof of the dorm." David, more serious and quiet. "Cleaning, guttering."

"Let's head that way. Maybe they need my help."

"You won't remember, will you?" Timmy asked. "Because you've damaged stuff inside your head."

"Yeah, I guess I have."

A truck pulled down the drive of Camp Hope. Beth. What in the world would she be doing there? The camp was too much like church for his sister's comfort.

"Is that Beth?" David stood next to him, leaning in slightly, his bare feet scrunching in the dirt.

"Yeah, it's Beth."

"Are you serious?" Timmy shouted. "She wouldn't come near here with a ten-foot pole."

Jason laughed, because that was pretty close to right. "Let's see what she wants."

"Do we hafta?" Timmy pulled loose from his hand. "We kind of wanted to play with tanks and stuff, or maybe play with you. But we don't want to talk to a girl."

"Fine, I'll catch up with you." Jason headed back in the direction of his sister. She was getting out of her truck and looked about as happy as Timmy had. "What's up, Sis?"

"Antibiotics?"

"Antibiotics?"

"For my horse. You were going to pick them up and bring them home. You drove past the house, so I thought I'd better run over here and see if you remembered."

If he remembered. He rubbed a hand over his face and tried to think back, to the remembering part. Nothing. He closed his eyes and worked backwards, retracing where he'd been. And he could only remember one thing, lavender and roses.

"Jason, this isn't good. You really need to go back to the neurologist." Beth walked him over to his truck. "I'll go with you."

"I know you would." He opened the door of the truck as his phone rang. Beth climbed in, he took the call. As she hunted through his truck, he walked away.

Beth chased after him, catching him as he ended the call.

"Who was that?" She held the antibiotics up for him to see. "You remembered."

"That's good to know." He slipped the phone

into his pocket. "That was Roy Cummings. He wanted to know how I'm feeling and if I plan on getting back on tour."

"You can't." Beth shook her head. "Jason, you can't be thinking about it, can you?"

"I don't know. What else can I do, Beth? I'm a bull rider."

"You're a bull rider who suffered a serious head injury. You could get hurt worse. You could…"

Jason hugged her. "I know what could happen. I've talked to the sports medicine team. I've talked to the neurologist. My short-term memory is damaged, Beth. I know all that. But I also know that I can't throw it all away without trying to fight back."

"Why do you need this so much?" Beth glanced over her shoulder at a car coming up the drive. "Seriously, Jason, you have your ranch. You have this community."

Jason couldn't give her the answer she wanted.

All his friends were settling down, having families and building lives. And he couldn't remember going to the store for his sister.

A car pulled up the drive and parked. Etta's car. He couldn't remember the name of the woman getting out of the passenger's side. But he knew her.

"Is that the reason you had to go to Etta's this morning?"

He had no trouble remembering his sister, standing there staring at him, a smirk of a smile on her face. He pulled the paper out of his pocket and glanced over it, at the note telling him to go to the feed store and at the bottom of the page, the name Alyson.

"Yeah, I think so. That's Alyson. She's Etta's granddaughter."

"Some things haven't changed. You can still remember a woman's name." She watched Etta and her granddaughter. "But since she's with Etta, I think you should be careful. Break her heart and Etta will break your neck."

"You think?"

"I'm pretty sure of it. Did you know that someone bought the old church on Back Street?"

"I guess I didn't know that."

The church they had attended with their mother. It had been closed down for years. People had left the small country church behind, looking for more. If he closed his eyes, he could remember in detail the inside of that old building. He could remember how it felt to sit next to his mom and sing "In the Garden."

The fact that church interested his sister was more of a surprise than the fact that someone had bought the building. Their father had jerked her out of church about ten years ago and she hadn't been back. Now he thought she stayed away because of the recent past, not the distant.

"The sign in front of it says Sold." She looked up at him, and then glanced back at Etta. "She looks like Andie."

"She's Andie's sister. I think they might be twins." He glanced down and smiled. "How's that for short-term?"

"Good. When did Etta get home?"

"I didn't say the memory was perfect." He pointed to his head. "Remember, head injury."

"You need a keeper."

"I'm starting to realize that." He definitely needed someone to keep him on track until his memory returned to normal. If it ever did. He paused at that thought. Not long enough to let it get to him. He was an expert at not letting things get to him. "Are you here to work?"

"You know I'm not. Jas, do you want me to drive you home?"

"Why would I need that?"

"You look pale and you're limping."

"I'm good."

"Yeah, you're always good." She hugged him. "I'm heading home. Call if you need me."

She took the paper from his hand and wrote on it. "In case you forget."

"I won't forget."

As she walked away, he turned back to Etta and Alyson. Something had changed. He studied the woman in worn jeans, a T-shirt and flip-flops. He didn't remember her being like that. He remembered cashmere. And pink.

Of course Alyson's grandmother led her directly to Jason Bradshaw. In the few hours the two had spent together, Alyson had learned that her grandmother did her own thing.

On the way to Grove, they had talked about how a younger Etta had backpacked across Europe, lived in a commune during the early seventies, and then found Jesus in a real way and settled in Dawson with Henry Forester.

He died when her children were young and she started a business making tie-dyed clothing.

And now she was making a beeline for Jason Bradshaw, holding tight to Alyson's wrist, as if she thought her granddaughter might try to escape. And Alyson couldn't lie and say the thought hadn't crossed her mind.

"What is it we need to do here, at the camp?" Alyson thought her question might pull her grandmother back and get her on track.

"Well, we're going to check on Jason and then we're going to ask Jenna and Adam what we can do to help them get started next week when the first campers arrive."

"I see." Alyson had never been to camp, and now she was going to volunteer at one.

"Jas, honey, are you here to work?"

"I think I probably am." He winked at Alyson. She looked away, scanning the camp, the buildings, the fields.

"There's Jenna and the guys." Etta pointed to a woman with a round belly. There were two men with her. One had a protective arm around her waist. The other was stepping onto a ladder.

"She sure looks pretty pregnant." Etta smiled at Jason, not at Alyson. "Adam's a lucky guy."

"I'm happy for them, Etta."

"I know you are, but a few of us thought…"

He limped ahead of them, ignoring her grandmother's unspoken question about what people thought. But Alyson wanted to know. What had people thought? Had there been something between Jason and Jenna?

"They were only friends," Etta answered. "I just don't know what's wrong with that boy. He's never had a serious relationship. Always been that way."

"Maybe he doesn't want to get serious with anyone." It made sense to Alyson. So did changing the subject, but something else she'd learned about her grandmother was that Etta was relentless.

"Well, that doesn't even make sense. Of course he wants to get serious with someone." Etta made a face, drawing in her brows and scrunching her mouth and nose. "Why aren't you married?"

"I..."

"Well?"

"I was engaged."

"I see." Etta stopped walking. "Is that why you're here?"

"No, not really. I mean, it's part of it. I wanted to find you."

"And you wanted to find a place to hide. We're more than a shelter in the storm, Alyson, we're your family. We're going to be here, even when the storm passes. Make sure you remember that."

Alyson nodded. "I know. And I'm not here to hide. I'm here because I found you."

As they approached the group gathered at the corner of the dorm, Jason spoke to the woman, and then glanced toward Alyson and Etta. She couldn't hear what they were saying, but he looked away, and he looked uncomfortable.

"Etta, you're back." The woman, round and pregnant, hugged Alyson's grandmother.

"Well, of course I am. I had a surprise waiting for me." Etta slipped an arm through Alyson's. "Honey, this is Jenna, her handsome husband Adam Mackenzie. And that guy on the ladder is her brother, Clint."

"Nice to meet you all."

"Are you here for long?" Jenna spoke, her hand going to her belly.

"I'm not sure."

Etta shot her a look that questioned her answer, but Alyson couldn't explain. How could she give answers when she had no idea what her future held? She couldn't explain to her grandmother about her fears.

For a little while she wanted to be a girl from Dawson. She might want to be that person forever. But wanting didn't undo the realities of her life and a schedule that couldn't be undone.

Jason smiled at her, making her answer okay. He winked and his hand went to the ladder, shaking it a little, distracting the people looking at her, waiting for answers. Clint Cameron grabbed the edge of the roof that he was working on.

"Give a guy a break when he's standing on a ladder."

Jason looked up, pushing his hat back. "Sorry, Clint, just making sure it's steady."

"Right." Clint took another step up the ladder. "Try to hold it steady."

"Jenna, we're here to volunteer." Etta stepped closer to the group, pulling Alyson with her. "I know you've got camp starting on Monday. If you need unskilled labor, Alyson and I will be here."

"We can always use help." Jenna's smile was sweet, and she held on to her husband as if he was the best thing in the world. "I know that I'm not going to be a lot of use, so we could really use kitchen help."

"Kitchen would be great." Etta wrapped an arm around Alyson's shoulders and squeezed. "It'll be fun, won't it?"

Alyson made a weak attempt at smiling and Jason laughed. He shot her a look and shook his head. "I don't know if you want her in your kitchen."

"Why is that?"

"I don't remember a lot, but I do remember putting out a fire in Etta's kitchen."

"Kittens, fires—what in the world kind of trouble are you going to drag out of your hat tomorrow?" Etta asked, still holding Alyson close.

"I'm sure she can think of something." Jason held the ladder as Clint climbed down.

"Are *you* going to work in the kitchen?" Alyson directed the question at Jason, who was standing by the ladder, pretending it wasn't holding him up. She knew that it was. She had him figured out. He deflected to keep the focus off him.

She had realized a long time ago that she learned more watching than she did talking.

"I'm not sure what I'll be doing." Jason stepped away from the ladder.

"Are you going back on tour when the doctor gives you the okay?" Clint asked as he pulled off work gloves. "We could really use your help here, with the junior rodeo at the end of camp."

Jason shrugged. "I've been thinking about it. If I can go on tour, I probably will. I need to get on some practice bulls and see how it feels. Or I might try some smaller, local events."

"You can't," Jenna spoke up and Alyson wanted to agree, even if it wasn't her business. "Jason, come on, is it really worth it?"

"Jenna, I don't have a family. I'm a bull rider."

"I hope you'll think about this," Jenna spoke softly, and then seemed to let it go.

Alyson listened but she wasn't going to

comment on someone else's career, not when her own was going down the drain fast. And she didn't want them to know that she'd fed her curiosity about Jason Bradshaw.

She'd used her computer to search his name and information about his accident. He'd been unconscious when they took him from the arena. He hadn't regained consciousness for twelve hours. He had suffered a traumatic brain injury with symptoms that included short-term memory loss, headaches and dizziness.

He was the kind of person who faced his fears. She had never been that type of person.

But she was here, she reminded herself. She was in Oklahoma. She had left Boston, driven for two days, and made it here. She hadn't asked anyone's opinion, hadn't cleared it with anyone. She had just left.

Because her life wasn't about fear, or playing the piano. This was her life, too. She was Alyson Forester. And she knew that, deep down inside, she was strong.

She was strong enough to meet the gaze of a cowboy with a slightly wicked smile and brown eyes that flashed with humor when he winked at her.

Chapter Five

He had to stop flirting with Alyson Anderson. Jason watched her walk away with Etta and Jenna. The three of them were going to the kitchen to talk about what they should expect next week. He didn't look away, not even when Clint cleared his throat to get his attention.

"If you mess with that, Etta will be on your doorstep with a shotgun," Adam warned.

"I know." Jason turned back to the two other men and ignored the strong desire to seek Alyson out, to get to know her better. "What's up with the camp?"

"We're going to have a great summer, Jason. We'd really like for you to be part of this." Adam nodded in the direction of the barns and stable. "Come on out and I'll show you what we're working on. Clint?"

"I'm going to get these gutters finished and head home."

"Okay, thanks. I'll see you tomorrow." Adam started walking and Jason followed.

They stopped at the gate next to the barn. Jason leaned against the top rail and looked out at the field, and then in the direction of the indoor arena.

"You've come a long way with this place."

Jason watched the two dozen horses grazing in the field, cows with calves a short distance away. A little over a year ago, there had been nothing here but a few of the buildings. Adam had arrived to find the place half-finished and the money to finish the rest had been spent by his cousin.

What a difference a year could make.

And a year ago, Jason was working hard, fast on the track for a world title. This should have been his year. It probably would have been, if it hadn't been for the wreck of the season that ended with him in the hospital for a couple of weeks.

Adam Mackenzie wanted him here, working at Camp Hope. It meant more than people realized. It meant staying, being involved. A guy couldn't do something like this halfway, without total commitment.

Of course, a guy had to be pretty committed to staying full time on the back of a bull, too.

Maybe he was better at commitment than he realized.

Or maybe it was because bulls weren't people and didn't expect much from him.

He figured he was an expert at being detached. He'd learned it from the best, his father. Detachment was not getting too close to a mother that fought cancer for a dozen years. Because Jason had known, even before anyone had said it, that he wouldn't always have her.

He remembered the little ways he had pushed her out of his life. And now he recognized that he'd been a kid trying to protect himself from being hurt.

She had always pushed right back, insisting on hugging him when he was scared, insisting on being at school programs. Later, close to the end, she had talked to him about not being afraid to love someone.

He shook past that thought because it hadn't gotten any easier over the years. He'd become an expert at being unattached. There were exceptions, he realized. Beth, of course, his sister had always counted on him. They'd relied on each other.

And Jenna. She had needed a friend and he'd

been there for her. And she'd figured out a few of his secrets along the way.

"Adam, this camp is a big deal and you know I want to support you." Jason let his gaze wander—to the dorms, to the steeple of the open-air chapel.

"Yeah, I know. But we're looking for more than a check, Jason."

"Right." A rangy-looking colt walked up to the fence, inching his nose out. Jason scratched the horse's face and rubbed its neck. "That's about the ugliest horse I think I've ever seen."

Adam laughed. "Yeah, he's Jenna's favorite. Some spooky mare of hers had this thing last fall."

"She would like it." Jason patted the horse's neck one last time and turned away from the fence. "I'll do what I can for the camp. I have a doctor's appointment next week. I've got people pressuring me about riding next month. And then I've got people telling me I'd be crazy to ride."

"And the sponsors always have to be happy." Adam walked next to him, slowing his mammoth stride. "I get that."

"Yeah, I know you do."

"I won't pressure you, I just want you to know that there's a spot for you if you decide this is where you're supposed to be." Adam turned and they started the walk back to the main campus area.

Jenna was waiting for them at the dining hall. The boys were playing on the swing that hung from the oak tree nearby. She watched, but her hand kept going to her belly.

Jason shoved aside the moment of envy. Not because Adam had Jenna, but for what the two of them shared. How could he envy something he had never wanted?

It was the epidemic of love and marriage that was getting to him. Everyone had caught the illness, and he was the last one with any immunity. Cody, Adam, Clint—they were all married now with kids, or kids on the way. Clint and Willow were working on adopting child number two.

There were so many happy-ever-afters, a single guy had to keep his guard up. It kind of gave him the willies when he thought about it.

"How's your memory?" Adam asked as they sat down on the bench next to Jenna.

"Another reason you wouldn't want me working with kids. What if I put one on a horse and forgot he couldn't ride. Or forgot that the horse wasn't broke." He tried to smile, as if it were a joke.

Jenna patted his shoulder. "We'll get you a helper."

"Thanks." Jason stretched, straightening his leg out and taking a deep breath when the pain hit. Adam had asked him a question. "My memory is improving, though."

He had remembered Alyson. More specifically, he remembered her perfume, and a cashmere sweater.

"I should head home." Jason stood up. "I'll pray about helping."

He lifted his hand in farewell and walked across the big lawn toward his truck. He worked up a memory of Alyson in blue jeans, flip-flops and a T-shirt. She hadn't been dressed like that the day he first saw her.

A memory had never felt so good. But some strange twist to his gut told him the memory was dangerous.

After talking to Jenna, Alyson and Etta stopped at the Mad Cow. Alyson walked through the door of the café with her grandmother. It felt better than it had the previous evenings, when she'd come here alone. This time people smiled. They still stared, but it wasn't like before when everyone was trying to figure who she was and why she was in their town.

Today she was one of them. Kind of.

And she'd never been that before. At least not like this. She'd been in a group of children who all had spectacular musical gifts, so much so that people would pay to see them, to listen to their music.

"You okay?" Etta gave her a gentle push toward a booth in the corner, pausing for a moment to say hello to a friend and introduce her. And wasn't it wonderful to have her in town?

Alyson smiled, but her lips trembled and it was hard to breathe.

"Hold it together, kiddo." Etta whispered as they sat down on opposite sides of the booth.

Alyson blinked to clear her vision. It was the restaurant that caused a little bit of a light-headed feeling. The walls were painted with black-and-white splotches, like the hide of a cow. The booths were black. The tabletops were black Formica. And the tiles on the floor, black and white.

Vera, owner of the Mad Cow, came out of the kitchen carrying an order pad and two menus. She wore black pants, a white top and black-and-white spotted boots.

"Etta, great to have you back in town. And wasn't this a wonderful surprise? Alyson is back with us. Remember how she loved chocolate ice cream when she was a little thing? Goodness, always neat and tidy, too. And Andie couldn't ever eat a bowl of ice cream without getting half of it on her face or clothes."

Alyson blinked a few times, because last night Vera had been pleasant, but hadn't shared personal stories with her. Even her grandmother had been vague on personal stories. But this story—maybe it explained why Andie wouldn't have survived their mother.

"She's still pretty neat and tidy, Vera." Etta smiled at Alyson. "But from the looks of my kitchen, cooking isn't one of her skills."

"That's okay. She has other gifts." Vera patted her shoulder. "What can I get you ladies for supper?"

Alyson started to order a salad, but her grandmother shot her a look. "Good heavens, child, do you really want to eat a salad when you could have Vera's chicken fried steak, smothered in gravy?"

It sounded like an artery-clogging special to Alyson. But her mouth watered and her body chanted something that sounded like, Must. Have. Carbs.

And she agreed. She nodded. "I'll take it."

Vera smiled big and scribbled on the order pad. "Now that's more like it, sweetheart. A person can't live on salad alone. You having the same, Etta?"

"No, honey, I'm having her salad."

Vera laughed. "So, does Andie know her sister is home?"

"I called her this morning." Etta smiled and Alyson got the impression there was more to the call.

When Vera walked away, Etta stopped smiling. "There's something you learn in a town like Dawson. You don't ever give all the facts unless you want everyone to know your business."

"So what is our business?"

Etta poured sugar in her coffee and stirred it. "I called, but Andie didn't answer. She doesn't always."

"Oh."

"But she'll be home. She'll see my number on the caller ID and she'll call." Etta smiled big, as if everything was perfect, but it wasn't.

Alyson smiled back, but apprehension tugged at her stomach and she couldn't believe she was about to eat chicken fried steak smothered in gravy.

There were too many thoughts racing through her mind. She was thinking about Andie, about seeing a sister she hadn't seen since they were not quite three years old. And she couldn't help but think about Jason Bradshaw.

He was the last thing she should have been thinking about. She'd been dumped a month ago. She'd fallen apart, walking off the stage halfway through a concert, leaving a stunned symphony orchestra trying to pick up the pieces of a shattered performance.

The next day she'd read the article about what how she'd had a nervous breakdown. But she hadn't. It had been just the opposite. She had finally walked away from something that she should have walked away from years ago.

Jason woke up the next morning with a pretty clear head and notes next to his bed telling him what he needed to do that day. After a cup of coffee, he walked out to the barn. His dad was coming out with an old saddle.

"What do you need me to do today?" Jason glanced at his watch. The notebook had outlined chores at his own place, a trip to town and stopping by Camp Hope.

"I can't think of a thing." Buck Bradshaw tossed the saddle into the Dumpster next to the barn. "Been meaning to throw that thing away for ages."

A thirty-year-old saddle that had belonged

to Jason's mother. The two men didn't discuss it, just went on. That's how they dealt with things in their family. Jason's dad probably hadn't planned on anyone seeing him throw the saddle in the trash.

But why now? Jason didn't ask questions. He wouldn't have gotten answers anyway.

"How you feeling?" Buck paused at the door to the barn.

"Feeling good, Dad." Jason glanced one last time at the Dumpster. "I need to run into town, get a few things done. If you need me, just call."

"I'll do that."

Jason was heading down the drive when he saw Andie driving toward town, her truck pulling the horse trailer with the living quarters that she spent most of her time in.

He eased onto the road and followed her. Not the best move—he knew that. He should have driven on out to Camp Hope. He had it on his notepad. He had talked to Adam yesterday and promised to pray about working at the camp.

And Alyson's name was written on the bottom of that page. Etta's other granddaughter. He hadn't forgotten her.

He almost wished he could. If he could forget her, he could drive on past Etta's. He could take a side road that would lead him to

Camp Hope and away from a situation that wasn't going to be pretty.

This had to be from the brain injury, this sudden need to be involved in everything, and his own crazy inability to walk away. It had nothing to do with a woman who reminded him of a summer day, kind of breezy, warm and easy to be around.

She even smelled like a summer day.

She was Andie's sister. And Andie was about to get the surprise of her life. There was no telling what she'd do when she walked through the doors and saw Alyson in her home, with their grandmother. People assumed life didn't bother Andie. Jason knew better.

The truck and trailer ahead of him turned into the driveway at Etta's and pulled down to the barn. He stopped next to the house and got out of his truck. As he walked, Andie jumped down out of her truck. It took him by surprise, how much she looked like her twin. He hadn't seen it before. They weren't identical, but they were close.

Andie was tough. She was country, the real deal, with her jeans tucked into leather boots, her T-shirt said something about being raised country. Her soft edges were hidden by a sharp personality, a sharp attitude.

"What are you doing here so early?" She walked back to the end of the horse trailer, sprang the latch and then flipped up the bar that kept the doors safely latched.

"Saw you driving by." Thought she might need a friend. He doubted that now.

"Cool." She walked into the empty side of the trailer, down to the end, where her horse was tied. She pulled the lead rope and freed him. "Back up."

The horse obeyed. When he backed out of the trailer, Andie had the lead rope. Her gaze shifted, to the back door of the house. Her eyes widened. Jason waited.

"What's she doing here?" Those were Alyson's sister's first words to her in over twenty-five years. So much for happy family reunions.

"She's found us." Etta said, reserved, smiling. "She found out who she is and she came looking for us."

Andie stared and Alyson waited, not knowing what to do. At least having a twin wasn't a surprise for Andie. Alyson's gaze shot to Jason Bradshaw and she wondered why he was there. For her sister, no doubt. They'd always known each other. They were friends.

And now, Alyson knew that she was the one

who wasn't supposed to be here. Andie sighed and held her horse close. Andie, who had had this life, these people, their father, the horses and a childhood.

"Andie, I'm glad you're home. I've been hoping…" Etta started.

Andie shook her head. "Right. I need to put my horse up. He's had a long trip."

Alyson made a move to follow her sister but a hand on her arm stopped her. Jason's hand. "Give her a few minutes alone. You've had a few days to adjust. She needs a little time, too."

"Okay." Alyson watched Andie walk through the doors of the barn and disappear into the darkness.

And she knew what her sister was feeling. She knew the emptiness. She knew betrayal, and the feeling that everyone knew something she didn't. It was a deep down hurt. Alyson felt it, too.

"How about a cup of coffee, Jason?" Etta, quick to get it together again. Her outfit today was jeans and a tie-dyed T-shirt. Her lavender/gray hair was held back with a scarf. "Did you already eat?"

"I had coffee, but I need to head out to Camp Hope." He pulled a notebook out of his pocket and Alyson smiled as he read it off to them. "Camp Hope, a bridle that Dad ordered, and dog food. If I don't see you all today, I'm sure I'll see you at church tomorrow."

Church. Alyson watched him walk away and she had another moment of not knowing what to do. Church? She glanced from her grandmother to the barn. Her sister did needlepoint verses. She probably understood faith.

Jason pulled out of the drive, waving as he took off down the road. Andie was still taking care of her horse. Or maybe waiting it out until they were gone.

Etta looked at the barn, and then back to Alyson. "We might as well go inside and wait. I guess I should have left a message on her phone, but I didn't want to tell her like that."

Alyson nodded because she didn't know what to say. She followed Etta to the house. Her grandmother had stirred up bread dough earlier and now she dumped it out on a cutting board. Alyson was pouring herself a second cup of coffee when Andie walked through the back door, the screen banging softly as it closed behind her.

Etta turned to smile. She was kneading the dough, the white glump sticking to her hands and the cutting board. Alyson sat down on a stool to watch, and to wait for her sister to say something.

Andie poured herself a cup of coffee,

spooned in several spoons of sugar and looked from her grandmother to Alyson. She shook her head and then took a sip of the coffee.

"So, you're back." Andie set the cup down and backed up to the counter. With hands braced on the edge of the countertop, she hopped once and sat. Etta shot her a look that didn't seem to stop her.

"I guess I'm back. It happened suddenly, finding out about my family here. And then learning that I had a sister, too." She had learned that from Jason.

"What does that mean?" Andie reached for her coffee, and Etta supplied the answer, dough sticking to her hands.

"Alyson didn't know about us. She found out by accident."

"She didn't tell you about us?" Andie stared, and then she shook her head. "She didn't tell you that she took the perfect kid and left behind the defective one?"

"That's enough." Etta shot Andie a look. She was pulling dough off her hands. Finally, she walked over to the sink and used her arm to turn on the water. "We're family and we're going to treat each other with love and respect."

"Fine." Andie sighed. "Fine."

"I'm not sure what to say to you." Alyson

wasn't sure how to take a deep breath, how to move forward. "I don't know why you're angry with me."

"Because she chooses to be." Etta picked up a towel and flipped it at Andie's arm. "Choosing to act like this is all about her. And I'm telling you right now, Andie, you're twenty-eight, not eighteen."

"Fine, it isn't all about me." Andie smiled a tight smile.

Alyson couldn't smile. This was the rejection part she had feared. "I didn't do this to us."

Andie jumped down from the counter, landing on the floor. When she smiled this time, it was a little softer. "No, you didn't. You had no idea. How'd you finally find out?"

"I was looking for my bankbook. I'd left it on the desk in my, *our* mother's office."

"And you found us in the desk?"

"I found a box that contained my real birth certificate, adoption papers and a couple of other papers."

"Wow, our mother is a piece of work."

"She…" How did Alyson defend their mother after all that she'd done to them? How did she tell Andie that the person who had given birth to them had gentle moments, sometimes.

"Don't defend her." Andie's smile faded. "Don't do that, not after everything she's done."

"I'm not defending her, Andie." Alyson stood up. "I'm not her. I'm your sister. I came here because I wanted to know my family."

"Fine, you know us. This is it. It isn't fancy. We're just country people and we go to church on Sundays."

Etta cleared her throat.

Andie laughed, real laughter, and it shifted her features. Her blue eyes danced. "Etta goes to church on Sundays. I'm the rebel. If you stay, you can't have that position in the family. You'll have to find your own niche." Andie looked her over, top to bottom. "I think you're probably still the good one. And I have chores to do. So if you don't mind, I'm going to get busy and when you're tired of pretending you're one of us and ready to *be* one of us, you let me know and I'll find something for you to do."

Andie walked out and Alyson stood there with her cup of coffee, watching out the window as Andie walked across the lawn to the barn. She was long legged, taking long strides. She was a part of this place in a way Alyson only wished to be.

She rinsed her cup and set it in the sink,

ignoring Etta's knowing smile. "I'm going outside to help my sister with the chores."

When she reached the barn, Andie was waiting. She was leaning against the support post in the barn, messing with her fingernails. She looked up and smiled at Alyson.

"I thought that would get under your skin."

"Does this have to be our relationship?"

"Alyson, I got left here because you were the good one. You were the easy child. You didn't make messes. You probably even learned to read and I bet you can do long division without a calculator."

"Of course I…"

Andie looked away and Alyson got it. "She rejected me because I wasn't the perfect child. I don't think she could have known about my dyslexia, because my teachers didn't figure it out for years. They thought I was rebellious in school. But she knew that you were going to be special. You'd already proven that. And I've spent my life hearing it from everyone who met you—the sweetest toddler in the world. I can't live up to their perfect memories of my perfect twin."

Alyson reached for her sister, but Andie shook her head. "Don't. I'm not ready to hug you."

"Can I just say…"

Andie shook her head. "No, you can't. And even though I baited you to come down here, I don't want your help. I'm just cleaning out the trailer and I can do that alone. I need to be alone and I think Etta is probably ready to drive out to Camp Hope. Go with her."

Andie walked away and Alyson stood in the yard, watching her go. "I was just going to tell you that you had Etta. You had our father. And I've never been perfect."

But Andie didn't hear and Alyson didn't know if she'd ever listen. She turned back to the house, and Andie had been right. Etta was waiting.

Chapter Six

Jason walked through the stable, amazed by what Adam and Jenna had built in one year. They had built a place where dreams came true for kids who wouldn't ordinarily get to attend a summer camp, not one like Camp Hope.

And they wanted him to be a part of it.

In a couple of days a group of kids would arrive. He could stay here and teach those kids to ride, barrel race, rope calves and ride bulls.

He obviously wasn't going to be riding a bull for a while. So maybe it was worth thinking or praying about. Adam came out of the office, distracted.

"What's up?" Jason walked through the double doors and into the arena.

"I don't know. I've been trying to get hold of our accountant about some bills and a few checks from donors that haven't cleared." Adam shoved a few letters into his shirt pocket. "It's okay. Let's talk about camp."

"I'm thinking about it."

"It's a big commitment." Adam at least acknowledged that.

"Yeah, it is. And I haven't really thought about ending my bull-riding career this way."

"I get what you mean." Adam pointed to the mechanical bull at the end of the arena. "Were you wanting to try that thing out?"

Jason remembered Adam mentioning it. That was a huge improvement. "Yeah, I do. Give me a minute to stretch."

"Take your time."

Jason walked over to the mechanical bull. He would have touched his toes, but he couldn't manage it just yet. He raised his arms and swayed to the left and right. He bent his right knee, but the left pulled. He squinted against the sharp pain.

"Is he going to ride that?" It was Alyson's voice.

He turned and lifted his hat in greeting. "Yes. Do you want to give it a try?"

"Sorry, I'm pretty sure I'm not a bull rider."

He laughed at the look on her face. And then he remembered Andie.

"Andie came home, right?" He held his arms out and twisted right, and then left.

"Yes."

"You okay?" He stopped stretching and she nodded. "Sure you are."

Alyson approached, staring at the mechanical bull, and then turned her attention to him. Blue eyes caught and held his, and he forgot about pain.

"You're okay to do this?" Her gaze slid back to the bull.

"I'm good." Or at least he was about to find out if he was.

He climbed onto the mechanical bull and wrapped the leather around his hand, tight. He lifted his left arm and nodded once. Adam turned the machine on and controlled its moves. It bucked up and down, and then around.

Jason moved with the movement of the barrel. He kept his left arm up and his chin down. It wasn't easy, not as easy as it should have been. A mechanical bull didn't move like a real bull. It could do the unexpected, but it didn't take steps forward. It didn't come off the ground, all four legs in the air. It didn't land with a jarring thud that rattled a guy's brain.

But it did work him out. It did spin. It did buck. It didn't manage to unseat him. When it slowed to a stop, he climbed off. He stood there for a long second, waiting for the world to stop spinning. The vertigo shouldn't have lasted as long as it did.

Alyson headed his way. "Are you okay?"

He took off his hat and took a step toward her. "Of course. Do you want to give it a go?"

"Ride it?"

"That's what I mean." He liked the way she bit down on her bottom lip and studied the mechanical bull, her eyes narrowing as she considered his offer.

She nodded. "I think I can do that. You make it look easy."

He laughed. "It isn't easy."

He pulled off his glove and handed it to her. "Do I put this on?"

"That's the idea of it. And when you get on that thing, you hold with your legs. You keep your head down and you don't let your right arm get straight on you. The momentum can fling you off the back end if you let yourself get pulled back."

"If I ride this, I can be a bull rider?" She said it with a smile that made his head stop spinning for a second.

"Yeah, you can be a bull rider. Come on, let me help you get your hand tied in." Jason took her hand and led her across the padding that surrounded the mechanical bull.

She stopped before they reached it. He glanced sideways and she was breathing in, eyes closed. He held on to her hand and her fingers squeezed a little. "I can do this," she whispered.

"Of course you can. It's a mechanical bull. We're controlling it and we're not going to let it go crazy on you."

"I know."

"You don't have to."

"I do have to." She opened her eyes and managed a smile. "I'm ready."

She climbed on and he helped her get settled. She met his gaze and her eyes were bright, sparkling like blue topaz. He really wanted to kiss her. He wanted to pull her close and undo the clips that kept her blond hair in a tidy little knot at the nape of her neck. Instead, he pulled a few tendrils loose to frame her face and he stepped back.

He didn't know if he could get far enough away from her to feel safe.

"Remember what I said," he warned as he moved away.

"I can do this."

He nodded and walked away, because he understood. It was something she had to do. He glanced toward the box with the controls, ready to give Adam the signal. Adam was gone.

The two of them alone shouldn't have been a problem for Jason, but suddenly it was. Walking away from her, he battled a strong urge to hold her close and kiss her. He let out a sigh as he stepped behind the controls of the bull.

"Ready?" He smiled as he looked up at the woman on the back of the mechanical bull, her smile teetering on the edge of tears. But her chin was set at a stubborn angle. "Tuck your chin and put your left hand up. Use it for balance. And don't worry, I'm not going to let that bull get you down."

"It isn't a real bull." She called out and she did what he'd told her to do. Head down, hand up. "Go."

She was ready for this. Alyson's heart picked up speed as the bull started to move, and she had to focus, to concentrate on the way the thing moved. That was hard to do when her brain seemed to suddenly warp out, sending her mind on a field trip of some sort.

She couldn't stop thinking about a cowboy who had smiled at her, winking when she felt the most fear. She had never felt stronger.

She could do this.

Her brain whirled back to center, back to the task at hand. She could ride a bull. It jerked and spun. She kept her head down, but her arm above her head flung back, threatening to take her with it. She leaned a little, pulling it back.

"Don't touch the bull or you're disqualified." The words of warning came in wafts as she spun and she couldn't nod to let him know that she'd heard.

The mechanical bull, a barrel with a head and horns, twisted and bucked.

And then it stopped, and her heart was racing and her legs shook. It took her a few minutes to adjust to the end of the ride, to where she was. She was sitting on a mechanical bull. The big, open arena enclosed them, but outside was the vastness of the Oklahoma countryside.

"You okay?"

She turned and gave a short nod of her head. "I did it."

She slid off the back of the bull and her legs buckled a little. He was there to reach for her, his hands steady on her arms.

She knew how to anchor herself. She knew how to stay grounded and steady. But at that moment, reasoning fled. Grounded and steady were the last two things she wanted to be. She didn't want to be the person who planned every moment of her life—not today.

She wanted to experience life. And she wanted to experience what it was like to be held by a cowboy.

She looked into deep-brown eyes and he winked. She'd seen movies and read books. She played country music when no one was around to listen. Cowboys were good at holding a woman. She ignored other thoughts, that they were also good at breaking hearts, good at leaving, and not good at staying.

The cowboy standing toe to toe with her believed she was strong. He had allowed her that moment, to prove it to herself.

As she tried to get her thoughts together, his hands moved to the clip at the back of her neck and her hair came loose. He clipped it to the hem of her shirt and then his hands moved to the back of her neck, winding through her hair.

She could have stopped him, but she didn't. Instead, she leaned a little toward him, breathing in deep of a cowboy who smelled like soap and leather. His hands were gentle but calloused, brushing her neck.

"I like it better this way," he whispered as he leaned in.

And she felt everything, all at once. She wanted to tell him to wait, to let this moment be one she'd never forget, because she'd never really been kissed, not like she knew he would kiss her.

And before she could tell him, his lips touched hers and she was lost. He held her close, and everything changed, because she could only think about him, not anything else but being in his arms. She sighed and stopped thinking.

He whispered something she couldn't understand, and then he kissed her again.

Bull riding was nothing compared to that moment in the arms of a cowboy.

"I..." Jason didn't know what to say. He hadn't planned that.

He hadn't realized that it wouldn't be enough, that he wouldn't want to let her go. Ever.

That was a new experience for him, not wanting to let go.

He slid his hands around her back and drew her to him, holding her in a loose hug, and resting his cheek against the blond hair that he'd released from its clip.

He thought back to the kiss. He'd felt

that led to the dining hall and dorms, he saw Etta and Alyson getting in Etta's car, leaving.

"If you don't want to work in the kitchen, Jenna said they could use you in the stable. She thought you might like to work down there, with the horses," Etta said as she parked the car under her carport at the side of the house.

Alyson nodded but didn't know what to say. She could have said that she knew that Jason had decided to work at the camp, in the stable. She could even tell her grandmother that she didn't need the help of matchmakers.

Instead, she followed Etta up the sidewalk that was cracked in places, with grass and dandelions growing up in the broken areas. The kitten, banished from the house after it was caught sharpening its claws on an antique stool, ran from the shed, mewing for food.

More to comfort herself than the cat, Alyson scooped up the kitten and held it close. It purred loudly, working tiny claws in her shoulder as it snuggled close.

The back door opened and Andie walked out, her short hair catching in the light breeze. "There's cat puke in my room."

"Hi to you, too." Etta shot a look back at Alyson and the kitten. "You get to clean that up."

"I will."

Andie smiled a little. "I made chocolate chip cookies."

Etta shook her head. "I'm going to sit in my room with a book and the ceiling fan on. You two enjoy the cookies."

Alyson followed her sister into the house. The cookies were on a tray and there was a pitcher of iced tea. "I thought the two of you would be ready for a break."

Andie was considerate. It was crazy to learn this stuff about her sister now, when Alyson should have always known. They should have had a lifetime of knowing these things about one another.

They walked down the hall to the front door and onto the wide front porch with its lavender-painted wicker furniture. The sweet scent of roses and other flowers drifted on the breeze. But there wasn't much of a breeze. Andie sat down on the wicker chaise lounge and drew her knees up. Her feet were bare and she had a flower tattoo on her ankle.

Alyson looked around, at the wicker chairs and the porch swing. She picked the porch swing, facing her sister. She reached for a cookie and set her glass of tea on the table.

Jason drove by, his truck pulling an empty

horse trailer that rattled on the paved road. "Wonder where he's going," Andie mused as she lifted the glass to take a sip. And then she glanced at Alyson. "Why does the sight of Jason Bradshaw make you turn that lovely shade of pink?"

"It doesn't." Alyson didn't want to talk about Jason. She wanted to talk about two sisters who had lost so much of their lives together.

"You can stop looking at me with the big, sad eyes." Andie held her tea glass and stared out at the road.

"I'm not looking at you." Alyson sighed. "Okay, I am. You know, I don't remember you. I didn't have pictures. No one mentioned you to me."

"So you're saying that I had it better because I was aware that my sister was taken by our mother and I was left here."

"Was here such a bad place?"

"No, here was a great place. The idea that I wasn't good enough for our mother, that I wasn't smart enough or talented enough, that can kind of wound a kid and make her feel a little inferior."

"I know, and I'm sorry. But you have to understand, that wasn't my fault."

"No, Alyson, being a brilliant child prodigy wasn't your fault."

Alyson stood up, her insides trembling. She'd never been so mad in her life. She stood there staring at her sister, and Andie staring back.

"*Child* prodigy, Andie. I was a *child* with a gift. And now I'm just another piano player. I have no skills. I have no life. I played the piano. I graduated early. I've never been to a prom or a homecoming. Now I have to figure out where I belong."

"Figure it out. You're an adult. No one is going to tell you who you need to be."

But for twenty-eight years people had told her who to be, so finding herself now didn't seem like such an easy thing to do.

"You make it sound easy. But you've always known who you were."

"Yeah, I guess I did." Andie picked up another chocolate chip cookie. "But I think you know who you are. You must be a Forester, because you got mad and left."

Alyson smiled at that and she sat back down. "Yes, but I planned it for over a week."

"Yeah, I would have just jumped in the truck and left."

"I'm glad you're my sister." Alyson didn't say it too softly, because Andie obviously didn't do soft.

"Yeah, about that. I'm okay with having

you back, and I've missed having a sister. But what set you off? What suddenly sent you running?"

"We have a half sister named Laura, and a month ago she eloped with the man I thought I was going to marry."

"Ouch."

"Yeah, ouch. Too bad I don't miss him."

They both laughed, and it felt good to have that moment between the two of them, a moment that signified something, maybe healing.

"There are photo albums." Alyson loved those photo albums. She'd looked at them several times already, but not from Andie's perspective. "Would you look at them with me?"

"And take a trip down memory lane?" Pain hid within the sarcasm in Andie's tone.

"At least tell me something about our dad." Alyson swallowed. "Isn't there something you want to know about my life, about our mother, or your half sisters?"

"Soon, but not yet. It isn't easy, knowing the reason she left me. I've always known and I've always had that resentment."

Alyson smiled. "She didn't get an easy out, Andie. She didn't trade you for a perfect child, or perfect children. I'm dyslexic, too. It drove her crazy, trying to force me to learn the way my sisters learned. And they drove her crazy with bids for attention that you won't believe."

Andie smiled. "Okay, let's share."

"What was he like?" Alyson had to start there, with her father.

"Always lonely." Andie offered but she looked away and Alyson saw the moisture gather in her eyes. "He always missed her and you."

"But he loved you?" Alyson wanted it to be a fairy tale. She wanted to believe what she'd told herself on the drive here, that there was this perfect parent who had missed her. He would have been her hero.

"He loved me. He loved us both." Andie said it the way a person dismissed trivial facts. "But he started drinking when I was five. And if the car accident hadn't killed him, I think drinking would have."

Alyson sighed, because she had wanted to believe that things here were different. There were no fairy tales. "I'm sorry."

"Don't be. I wasn't unhappy. He loved me. Granny loved me. I grew up riding horses and pulling crazy stunts." Andie turned to sit on the side of the chair. "What did you do?"

"I…" Alyson thought back, to what she had done, something that sounded more exciting than hours at the piano, panic attacks before walking out onstage, or her mother telling her she was a disappointment. "I played in London for the queen."

Andie laughed. "I said, what did you do for *fun?*"

They both laughed. "I don't know if fun was allowed. While I played and performed, Dad—" She shook her head. "Gary would take Laura and Cindy places. I did see a lot of museums."

"If you're trying to make it sound bad so I won't be jealous, it's working."

"You have nothing to be jealous of." Alyson looked up as a truck approached. Jason Bradshaw driving by with a horse in the back of his trailer. "What's Jason like?"

"If you're a pianist with big, blue eyes, he's a big, macho prince charming. If not, he's the guy down the road that you've always liked, because he's always been funny, always been easy to get along with. His mom died years ago. His dad is difficult. His sister ran away. Kind of a typical family with normal problems."

"As opposed to a mom who took one kid and left the other?"

"He's broken a lot of hearts, Alyson. And then he got religious and broke a few more. Don't let him break yours. He's looking for a good Christian wife these days. I don't think either of us fit that description."

Alyson shrugged it off. "I don't plan on getting my heart broken, and I don't plan on falling in love."

She didn't know what to say about being a Christian. She had agreed to attend church with Etta tomorrow. When she thought about it, her stomach did a small flip. It did another flip when she thought about seeing Jason there.

Chapter Seven

Jason found a parking space near the doors of the church and got out, alone, as usual. Beth had quit going when she was a teenager and realized it made their father angry. Jason's dad had never been one to attend church, not even before. And in their world, *before* always meant before Elena Bradshaw died. They didn't talk about her death. They didn't really talk about her, or life without her.

Instead, Buck Bradshaw had created a new life for his family after his wife's death. She was gone, and he acted as if she had never been there. But she had, and the big hole in all their lives was evidence of the fact.

Jason was still thinking about the saddle that had gone in the Dumpster. It should have been thrown away years ago. Letting it go had to mean something.

He took the step from the parking lot to the sidewalk and bit back some inappropriate words. Roping yesterday and riding a green broke horse hadn't been a good idea. He'd given it a try and jammed his knee worse than before. The fact that his jeans barely fit over his swollen leg was a pretty good indication that he wasn't going to be able to put off surgery much longer.

But it would have to wait because he wasn't going to miss out helping with camp. Not now that he'd decided he should do this. He'd keep weight off it a couple of days and then deal with it.

"What's wrong with you?" A familiar voice. He turned and smiled at Etta. And Alyson. That felt good, remembering her name, and remembering that her being there probably meant something.

"What do you mean, what's wrong with me?"

"Aren't there crutches in your truck for a reason?" Etta walked over to the door of his truck and gave it a yank. She pulled out the wooden crutches and handed them to him. "Stop being so stubborn and take care of yourself."

"I'm taking care of myself." He winked at

Alyson. "I knew the two of you would be along to give me a hand."

"And if we hadn't, you would have fallen on your stubborn face." Etta nodded toward the church. "Head that way or we're going to be late."

"And that'll be my fault, too?" He mumbled, for Alyson's benefit. She laughed a little and he shot her a sideways glance, winking again, because he liked it when she turned that pretty shade of pink.

She was about the frilliest thing he'd ever seen, even in her new "country clothes." Her denim skirt swished around her ankles and her blouse was ruffled. She smelled so good, he wanted to slide up close to her and see…

Or maybe just yank his thoughts back into check and remember that he was at church and she was searching for herself, not a relationship.

The stairs going up to the church were narrow and had been there since before Dawson was a town. The ramp, a new addition, required by the state, ran alongside the building. Alyson walked behind him, up that long ramp. He wondered if she always did what she thought was the right thing. This time the right thing was not letting him fall on his face.

"I really can make it on my own." He

glanced back over his shoulder. Her gaze was down, studying the wood of the ramp.

"I know you can, but I thought—" she smiled up at him "—that I'd catch you if you fell."

He swallowed any fool reply that tried to slip out. He could tell her a hundred ways a man could fall, and it wasn't about hitting the ground. It was all about lace ruffles and perfume that wrapped around a guy's senses and drove him to sing the Lord's Prayer in his mind to keep his thoughts on holy things as he walked into church.

"You can catch me if I fall." He stood back, motioning with his hand for her to walk through the doors of the church ahead of him, and she didn't. Instead, she looked a little green, and he remembered panic attacks.

"Give me a minute." She glanced around, and people were watching.

He stepped closer, close enough that it became just the two of them, and he knew that people would talk. But in a town like Dawson, that's just what people did. He didn't mind giving them something to talk about.

"Deep breath, darlin'."

"Okay." She closed her eyes, inhaling. He wanted to put his arms around her, but then she'd be the only thing holding him up and they'd both fall.

He hummed the Lord's Prayer and took a careful step back, trying not to tangle his legs, the crutches and the people walking past them.

"Why do you keep humming?" She looked up, distracted, and he hadn't realized he'd hummed out loud.

"I'll explain it someday." The church bell rang. "Ready?"

"As I'll ever be."

Etta appeared in the vestibule. "I saved us a seat, but thought the two of you might have changed your minds about coming inside."

"We're here." Jason wondered if Etta knew that her granddaughter had panic attacks. "No Andie, I see."

Etta shook her head. "Of course not. She guilted Alyson into coming, but she backtracked as soon as we got close to being ready. She said she's going to pick up another horse today."

"Sounds like Andie." He sat down on the end of the pew and stretched his leg out into the aisle.

"What happened?" Alyson asked as she reached for a hymnal.

"Bull bucked me off."

"That was a month ago. And my name is Alyson."

He laughed a little, because of her quirky smile and the way her brows arched when she was being funny, and then the hint of shyness, as if she had found out something new about herself.

"I know. I promise, I'm not going to forget you, not again. And I really do remember what happened. I did some calf roping with a friend and when I jumped off a horse I was trying out, I twisted my knee. I already have some torn ligaments, so…"

"You'll need surgery."

"Probably so." He put a finger to his lips and she nodded, but she kept looking at him, not at the front of the church.

Alyson glanced away from the cowboy sitting next to her. She swallowed emotions that surfaced, unfamiliar and consuming. She reminded herself of how it felt to be the person Dan left because she didn't know how to enjoy life. That note had changed her life more than his leaving her had. That note had hurt, because it had been the truth. And it hadn't been her fault that she'd become this person who lived by a schedule.

The pianist missed a note. Alyson looked up, catching the problem, shuddering a little, and not meaning to. The woman was doing a great job. There was something about the song, the way it lifted to the rafters of that little church. It wasn't polished, it wasn't perfect, but it was moving.

She listened as they moved from a song about the earth not being home, to a song she knew well. As the worship leader sang the words, "It is well, with my soul," Alyson wondered, as she had never really wondered before, what that meant. Before it had been a beautiful song, a song the piano brought to life. And now, listening, she realized it was about life and having something stronger than oneself to rely on.

And she didn't know if she could ever live through disasters and sing that all was well with her soul. How did a person do that? How did a person find peace within their soul?

How could she ever find it when fear bounced around inside her, stealing any peace she managed to find, and bitterness welled up within her when she thought of the life she'd missed because of her mother's selfishness?

The message created more questions in her mind, more questions than she had answers for.

"Where are we going for lunch?" Etta asked as they walked out of church an hour later.

Alyson was still lost in the words of a song,

still trying to make sense of peace, and her grandmother was moving on, as if this was all normal, as if everyone should understand and get this faith, this God that seemed to be such a part of these people's lives.

They assumed that everyone got it, that it was easy, but it wasn't. Maybe that was her, overthinking again.

A hand touched hers, fingers lightly brushing. She looked up, and his eyes held understanding. He winked.

"You with us?" He leaned into the crutches and his mouth tightened.

"Should you go to the emergency room?"

"For what?" He really looked confused.

"You fell off a horse, remember?"

He laughed, "I haven't forgotten. I just don't know why I'd go to the E.R. for that."

"Because that's what people do when they're hurt."

"Not this cowboy. I'll take some aspirin, put some ice on it and tomorrow be good as gold."

"While the two of you are talking, I'm going into a diabetic coma here." Etta sighed.

"You aren't diabetic." Jason took an easy step forward. "And if you'll join me at the Mad Cow, I'll buy lunch."

"I'm not a diabetic, but I'm definitely tired

of waiting." Etta pulled keys out of her purse. "Alyson, can you drive him?"

"I got myself here, I think I can drive myself to the Mad Cow."

"And you'll wreck your truck and hurt someone."

Jason held his keys in a tight fist. "Etta, have you ridden in a five speed with your grand-daughter? I bet she can't drive a stick shift."

"She needs to learn and who better to teach her?"

"Might as well drive my truck." Jason handed over the keys and Alyson didn't want to take them. "She won't give up."

"I can't."

"You've got to." He winked and walked away. As Alyson stood on the sidewalk, trying to figure out what to do, he was tossing crutches into the back and opening the door.

Okay, she was driving a truck. She opened the driver's side door and stared at the cowboy sitting in the passenger seat, a cute grin on his too handsome face. Smug. He definitely looked smug.

She climbed in and sat behind the wheel. Her feet were miles from the gas and brake, and the added pedal, the clutch. She felt queasy as she stuck the key into the ignition.

She started to turn the key and he stopped her. "Foot on the clutch." He clicked his seat belt.

"Foot on clutch. Anything else?"

"Once it's started keep your foot on the clutch and shift into Reverse. And then give it a little gas and back up. Then you'll put your foot on the clutch again and shift into first."

"Got it."

Alyson started the truck, remembering to keep her foot on the clutch and then forgetting as she put the truck into reverse. It jumped, choked and died.

"This is so hard on my truck."

"We could sit here and Etta would get the hint."

"She's already gone." Jason smiled. "We could go to my place and have a picnic."

A picnic. Alyson tried to remember the last time she'd done anything like that. She was tempted, and she knew he was teasing. It was just suggested as a way to get back at Etta, not because he thought it might be a good idea.

"Do you want to go on a picnic?" Jason turned, resting against the passenger side door, his arm over the back of the seat.

"It would be fun, someday."

He pulled out his phone. "We'll invite Etta." He was serious. She tried to stop him but he held up a finger to silence her and dialed. She started the truck again, not sure what to do next, so she sat there. A car drove around them, the people inside it stared, shaking their heads.

And of course Etta didn't want to go on a picnic, but encouraged the two of them to go ahead. She'd meet with friends. Alyson sat there, listening to the conversation on speaker. A picnic with Jason.

He put the phone away. "Now let's switch places."

They were still sitting in front of the church and everyone else was gone. "I can drive."

"Not on your life." He unbuckled his seat belt. "I'll slide over there, you come over here."

"I'll come around."

"Just climb over here." He shook his head and grinned. "Never mind, get out and go around."

When she got in on the passenger side, Jason was starting the truck. He did it with ease, shifting without so much as a chug or cough from the engine. Alyson watched out the window as farms rolled past, including the one where he lived with his dad and sister.

"Where are we going?"

"My place."

"When do you think you'll move back?"

"Soon. My memory is better. I still have

headaches, some dizziness, but not as bad. It's little stuff now. Did I put the milk in the fridge, or mail the check for the electric bill? But every day is a little better. Maybe because I'm learning to cope better."

"You remember me."

"You're not short-term." He grinned. "I had to keep reminding myself of you. Even of that kiss."

She felt heat work its way up from her neck to her cheeks.

"That shouldn't have happened."

"I don't know why it shouldn't have happened, and I've reminded myself of it on a daily basis, so I won't forget that it was about the sweetest thing that ever happened to me."

"Do you really think you should ride a horse?" Alyson changed the subject with ease, and she didn't admit that she'd thought about him, and about that kiss, so often she was starting to question her sanity.

She was twenty-eight and she really thought this might be her first crush. And if that was the case, it would end. That's what happened to a crush. At least she wasn't sixteen, so it wouldn't break her heart when it was over.

She knew about being dumped. She'd just never been dumped by a cowboy.

* * *

"Why wouldn't I ride a horse?" Jason stopped the truck in front of the house he'd built a year earlier. The farmhouse design was clean, with white siding, a green metal roof and porches that held empty flower baskets. He should have hired someone to take care of the place. Maybe he had planned to and had forgotten.

At least he could smile about it now.

"Your knee." Alyson broke into his thoughts with what sounded like a random phrase.

"My knee?"

"You asked me why I thought you shouldn't ride a horse."

"And the answer is, my knee?" And she was probably right. "Come on in, we'll get our lunch together and, I guess we'll drive the truck back to the creek."

"You think?"

She was pretty in her ruffled Western shirt and denim skirt. She wasn't country, but she was trying it on for size. Maybe someday she'd grow into it. Maybe she'd find out who she was in Dawson.

Or maybe she'd find that she really loved the city and her life was there.

"I think maybe you're coming out of your shell, Cashmere." He opened the door and before he could hop to the bed of the truck, she was there with the crutches. "Thanks."

"You're welcome. And thank you for suggesting a picnic."

"Been a while?"

"So long I don't remember the last time."

He pulled the key out of his pocket and unlocked the front door. After pushing it open, he motioned her inside. The house smelled clean, but deserted. He had Beth to thank for that. The hardwood floors were swept and mopped, the furniture was dusted. His sister, always looking out for him.

"I like your house." Alyson stood in the center of the living room. The furniture was plaid, and big rugs covered the hardwood. She zeroed in on the piano in the corner of the room. His mother's.

She crossed the room, forgetting him, but he didn't mind. He watched as she stood in front of it, her hands hovered over the keys and then dropped to her sides. He joined her, leaning the crutches against the wall and taking a seat on the bench. While she stood frozen in that space next to him, he played something he remembered, that he didn't have to open a book to play.

She sat down next to him, a frightened foal, not quite ready for contact. He knew that look in her eyes, that longing for something, and fear of reaching for it.

"I didn't know you played." Her shoulder brushed his.

"My mom taught me."

"Your mom?"

He gave her a sideways glance and then back to the keys of the piano, smooth from use. When he played, he remembered his mom, how it had felt to sit next to her before she got sick.

He played a hymn from church and she touched the keys, playing with him. But then she stopped and he stopped, too.

"Why don't you play?" He closed the piano up, but they didn't move from the bench.

"I can't." She didn't look at him, and she didn't cry. "For twenty-five years the piano has been my life and for most of those twenty-five years, I've hated it. The pressure, the practice, the people staring at me. I wanted to be like all of the other girls. I wanted to be like my sister, Laura. I wanted to go on dates, hang out at the mall and dance at the prom."

"I understand."

She looked up, her blue eyes penetrating, asking questions, and shadowed with the pain of a life lived for other people. He understood. He'd been an adult his entire life. He'd helped his mother with her medication because his dad had hidden in the barn. He'd held his sister when she cried, because their parents couldn't. He'd told stories, made people laugh. He'd learned to cook, to teach his sister the things she needed to know about life.

But he'd told jokes to keep people smiling, to keep them from noticing how much they hurt, and how much he hurt.

And now this woman, a woman with her own stories, wanted him to share his.

"We should get ready to go. Before long it won't be lunch, it'll be supper." He grabbed the crutches and she stood, as if she was still waiting for answers.

He wasn't going there.

He'd take her on a picnic and help her find the kid who should have grown up in Dawson. He'd teach her to ride. He'd even break the buckskin and give him to her. He could do those things.

She followed him through the big dining room with the French doors that led onto the back porch with its stone fire pit and outdoor kitchen. She stopped to look outside and he went on to the kitchen. He was pulling food out of the fridge when she walked into the room.

"What can I do?" She leaned against the counter and watched.

"You can get the chips down." He nodded in the direction of the cabinets. "They're up there. And if you could get the basket out of the lower cabinet."

"You keep food here, even though you don't live here."

"I have to eat when I'm over here working."

"I see." She had the basket out and she set it on the cabinet. "Do you work over here a lot?"

"Every day. The animals have to be fed. I have horses that need to be taken care of. This really is all new to you, isn't it?"

"I've always lived in cities." She glanced out the window. He followed her gaze, seeing what she saw, but not the same way. This had always been his life. The cattle, the open land, the rodeos.

She had always been city.

He didn't want to connect too much, not when it felt as if he wouldn't want her gone, not tomorrow, or even next week. She reminded him of a bird that just passes through, on its way to wherever it's supposed to be.

He'd seen one of those birds last week. Beth had pointed it out, asked him if he'd ever seen anything like it. He hadn't. And the bird hadn't stayed. It was going north, back where it belonged.

He was a broken cowboy without a career. What did a guy like him offer a woman like her? Why was he even thinking like that?

He had a brain injury, of course. He was thinking crazy thoughts. A man did that when he looked death in the face. It made him think about the future, like he needed to fill it up with something.

She wasn't the thing he was going to fill his life with. No matter how good she looked in his kitchen. He nearly laughed at the idea of her in an apron, tossing frozen pizzas in the oven.

"You okay?" She was standing close, and he really didn't need close.

"Good to go." He grabbed the basket and she took it from him.

"I can get it." She held it in front of her.

"I'll leave these here." He leaned the crutches against the wall and took a painful step without them.

"Have you ever been called stubborn?" she asked as he tried to take the picnic basket.

"More than once." He had the basket and he took another step. She walked next to him. Okay, so he'd done something pretty bad this time. He could feel his knee give with each step.

"Oh, come on, this is crazy. Cowboy or not,

you have to use common sense." Alyson grabbed the crutches and came back with them.

"Cowboys have plenty of common sense." He exhaled and gave up on strong and whatever else he'd been trying to be.

Idiot came to mind.

"Okay, let's go, Cowboy."

She sashayed out the front door, carrying the picnic basket and maybe his heart. But no, he didn't give that away. He'd never given that away.

Alyson sat next to Jason as the truck bounced through the field in the direction of a copse of trees at the far edge of the field. She'd kept her gaze averted for a minute or two, but now she was watching him again.

She enjoyed watching him, had enjoyed it from the first day when he'd come around the corner of Etta's house, a cowboy in faded jeans and a sweat-stained T-shirt. He still looked like that cowboy, rugged with that grin that hit a girl in the midsection.

She'd never met anyone like him. Maybe that was the attraction. It was just the experience, the newness of it all. Maybe it wasn't about the cowboy at all.

Sitting next to him, she felt like the kind of

woman who could be strong. She felt like she could haul hay, break a horse, and hog-tie something. She felt like the kind of woman who cooked big meals on a Sunday afternoon.

She wasn't that woman, but he made her believe that about herself.

"You're quiet." He reached to turn down the radio, silencing a Kenny Chesney song about tractors and haylofts.

"I'm just thinking."

"About?"

Anything but him. Unfortunately, it wasn't working, this effort at distraction.

"You ask a lot of questions, but you don't talk about yourself."

His eyebrows shot up and he grinned. "That's because I'm a private kind of guy."

"Is that it?"

"Yeah, that's it. I don't like to share my stories."

"But I want to know them." She'd get to know him, bit by bit, Etta had said. That's how you found out a man's stories.

"I'm sure you do." He slowed as they got closer to the trees. She could see the creek and hear the crickets, or maybe grasshoppers. He stopped the truck.

They picked their way across ground that

was rough, with heavy clumps of grass and a few big rocks. The trees at the edge of the creek were small and some were topped, as if someone had chopped the tops out.

"What happened to the trees?"

"Storms. Tornadoes." He nodded to a spot near the edge of the creek. "You can put the blanket there."

He'd pulled a blanket out from behind the seat of his truck and given it to her to carry. Alyson spread the blanket and took the picnic basket that he'd lugged along in his right hand, hobbling with one crutch under his right arm.

"Are there fish in the creek?" She held his arm and he lowered himself down, stretching out on the blanket. And then what? Was she supposed to sit next to him? Or maybe lean against a tree?

"Sit down." He shook his head and laughed a little. "I don't know about you, but I'm about to starve and you want to play twenty questions. No, there aren't any fish in the creek. My mom was probably one of the kindest women I've ever known, and she fought a twelve-year battle with cancer. I'm the oldest of two kids, and my dad is emotionally detached."

Alyson bit down on her bottom lip and fought the sting of tears, because she understood now why stories should come in small pieces. And she got that sometimes a story didn't tell anything about a person. It was just facts.

"I'm sorry."

"Alyson, sit down and relax. This picnic is for you. Enjoy it."

She sat down next to him, pulling her knees up and hugging them close as she watched the creek. A hand touched her shoulder and she turned to look at him.

"I'm sorry, I'm not good at the whole 'kiss and tell' part of relationships."

"I didn't expect kiss and tell. I wondered about you playing the piano."

"How'd you know that I play?" He grinned, probably because her face lost all of its color. "Kidding."

"Cute."

"Thank you, Ma'am. I like to think I am." He leaned back on his elbows, a piece of grass between his teeth.

"I was talking about your sense of humor, not you." She pulled food out of the picnic basket. "You're definitely not cute."

He sat back up. "Really?"

"Really." She handed him the sandwich with mayo and took the one without for herself. "We should eat."

"I left the room when my mom was taken off life support."

His words stole her appetite. She put the sandwich back in the baggie. "I'm sorry."

"It was my choice. I couldn't watch her leave. I knew her faith. I knew that she believed she'd go to heaven. But man, I didn't want her to go. I was so angry with God for thinking He needed her more than us. She was the person who kept our family together. Even when she was sick."

"Jason, I..."

He shook his head. "Let's not, okay. You wanted to know. I told you. End of story."

"I didn't mean to force this out of you."

He took in a deep breath and his expression shifted. With a tenderness deep down in his brown eyes, he touched her cheek and his smile returned. "It isn't something I like to talk about, but you didn't force me. I wanted to tell you. I want you to know me."

She tried to make sense of those words. He wanted her to know him. As she was making sense, he was moving closer.

He slid a hand behind her neck and pulled her to him, touching his lips to hers, holding her there for a moment that felt like forever. It was one of those moments, the kind that felt as if you'd caught a butterfly in your hand, or seen a meteor fall to earth. It felt suspended in time, and yet, not long enough.

The kiss was as soft as a whisper on a summer night. Alyson didn't plan on it ending, but felt the cold air between them when it did.

"I want you to know me," he whispered again near her ear and then grazed her lips with another sweet kiss. She'd never been kissed like that before, not in a way that touched her heart, that changed what she believed about herself, and about the person holding her close.

Her heart was melting.

Cowboys knew the right words. Cowboys were good at making a girl believe they loved her more than anything. And hadn't Andie warned her about him? Jason Bradshaw didn't do long-term relationships.

Her phone rang and, dazed, she reached for it, answering it without looking at the caller ID.

"Well, it's about time you answered." Her mother's voice.

Cold water in her face couldn't have been more effective in bringing Alyson back to reality.

"Mom."

Jason didn't move away. He sat next to her, filling their paper plates with food and twisting the top off a bottle of water before setting it next to her. Her mother's voice, tense and cool, edged out the warmth of the afternoon.

"So, I take it you're in Dawson?"

"I am."

"You need to come home. You have concert dates. You have family obligations."

"Mom, no one wants to hear me play. I'm twenty-eight. I'm not a child prodigy anymore. You don't need me."

Her shelf life had expired. Her father had other prodigies on his client roster. And yet, the guilt was still there because it had always been about doing the right thing for her family. Playing, even when playing was the hardest thing in the world to do.

"Alyson, Oklahoma isn't your life. You're not one of them. You're my daughter, not his."

"He's gone, Mom. And I'm trying to decide if this is my life."

Because she was suspended between who she had always been, and this new person she wanted to be, the person who made her own decisions, and kissed a cowboy until she couldn't breathe.

Chapter Eight

On Wednesday afternoon, the third day of camp, Jason stood next to a little gray mare as a boy with boots a size too big and a cowboy hat falling over his eyes swung himself into the saddle, nearly falling over the other side.

"Careful there, Hoss." Jason grabbed the boy by the arm and smiled at the gap-toothed kid. "You can't be like Jell-O. You've got to keep your back straight without being stiff and keep your arms tucked to your side. No spaghetti arms, okay?"

The boy nodded and Jason smiled again. The kid was shaking like a sapling in a storm.

"What's your name?" Jason adjusted the stirrups and then fixed the reins in the kid's hands. He had probably asked the kid his name three times, but eventually it would stick.

"Bobby."

"Well, Bobby, this is Cheerio. She's a pretty good little horse and she's never thrown anyone. The two of you are going to be good friends."

"Okay."

"But you have to breathe a little, okay? 'Cause if you pass out, you're gonna fall off."

"Okay."

Jason led the boy to the arena where four other kids were already walking their horses around the perimeter of the enclosure. He gave the horse a little pat on the rump, the boy jumped and the horse took off at a sedate walk.

He'd already given them all pointers on commands and how to keep their seat. A few had some experience. Some claimed experience they didn't have. He leaned on the gate and watched, but his gaze traveled to the dining hall.

Alyson had worked in the kitchen for the last few days. He'd seen her at lunchtime, serving chicken nuggets and salad to the campers and staff. She had smiled at each one of those kids, and he knew how that smile made them feel. It probably made them all feel like a five-year-old with the greatest kindergarten teacher in the world.

But she hadn't talked to him. Their gazes had connected, but she'd looked away and he'd pushed his tray off the end of the counter. Salad and nuggets had gone everywhere and the kids had gotten a great laugh over the mishap.

He shook his head and gathered his wits, because he had kids on horses and he didn't have room in his mind for them and Alyson. It was better, thinking about the campers, the sun beating down on his back, and a youth rodeo. Anything but a woman.

"How's it going?" Adam Mackenzie walked up, his hat off and his hair plastered to his head.

"Hot, isn't it?"

Adam nodded. "I've been chasing two boys around the yard, trying to get some kind of little snake away from them."

"But you love it."

"Yeah, I do." Adam rubbed his brow with his sleeve and settled his hat back in place. "How's it going?"

"Pretty good. I mean, you're not going to have a lot of problems with horses like these."

"What about your knee?"

"Good to go." Jason didn't look at the other man. He kept his focus on the kids, on the horses, watching for problems.

"Right. What do you think about this group? Can we pull off a showdeo at the end of the two weeks?"

A showdeo. A combination between a rodeo and a horse show. They would have steer riding, pole bending, egg relay and a Western pleasure class. If he had the kids with the ability, they might try roping.

Jason shrugged. "I think so. I'm going to work with a few of the more skilled riders this afternoon. I have a couple who think they can learn to rope."

"You're going to build Rome in a day?"

"I'm going to turn these kids into rodeo stars in two weeks."

"I don't doubt you will. Jenna suggested you let Alyson help you out. She looks a little lost in the kitchen."

"And you think she'll be better off working with the horses?" Jason knew this game, and he wasn't playing.

He'd found out a long time ago that controlling situations solved a lot of problems before they happened. Walk away from an argument, no fight. Walk away from the girl, no problems when she got sick of you or you got tired of her. Walk out the door of the hospital room...

And pretend it never happened, that his mother hadn't lost her life with the turn of a switch.

He'd been accused of not letting himself feel.

And Sunday afternoon he'd learned that maybe people were right. Because Sunday, he'd felt everything. He wasn't about to admit that what he'd felt the most was scared to death.

For a guy who rode bulls for a living, that was a little unnerving.

"I think Alyson would like working out here." Adam cleared his throat a little. "I didn't really think you'd mind."

Jason laughed. "Thanks, but no thanks. I have enough problems keeping focused without having to keep her out of trouble."

"I'll pass that on. You know your objections are only going to make the women push harder, right?"

"Yeah, I get that." Jason shifted his weight to his good leg. "But maybe you could tell them to give me a break. No sense in having a woman feel forgotten. That wouldn't be good for her self-esteem."

"That's a good point." Adam stepped away from the gate. "I need to get a few things done in the office. Yell if you need help."

"Will do. It's time for this lesson to end. I'm going to let them trot a little, so they feel like they've done something."

"Thanks, Jason. This program will be better with you involved."

"I hope."

Jason strode into the arena and called the kids to the center. After a few minutes of instruction he turned them loose. Smiles split across serious faces when he gave the nod and they loosened the reins and gave their horses the nudge to move them at a faster gait. He laughed a little because several of them looked as if they'd bounce right off the back end of their horses if he didn't stop them soon.

But he remembered being a kid and escaping on the back of a horse. And these kids needed the escape, probably more than he ever had.

As he ended their lesson, his gaze swept across the open field, catching sight of movement. Alyson walked down the hill to the chapel and he wondered why.

Alyson walked through the open doors at the end of the chapel and stood for a moment in the dimly lit entrance. The building had a roof and screened walls to let the breeze flow through.

At the front, behind the pulpit was a giant cross. She stared at the cross, not really getting it, and yet…

It ached inside her heart, not understanding what everyone else believed and held on to. And she needed something. She needed something more than herself and something more than her career.

She reached into her pocket and pulled out her phone. She pushed the button that turned it off. She couldn't take another call from her mother, more pressure, more guilt.

Alyson walked down the aisle to the front of the chapel. She sneaked a look around and hoped no one would be upset with her for being here. But when she'd left the kitchen, needing to be alone, to get away, the chapel had seemed like the place to go.

Last night she had sat in here with Etta, at the back, listening to Pastor Todd, the camp minister. He'd told funny stories, drawing the kids in with laughter. And then he'd brought them to a point where they understood faith, understood the point of a Father's love. An unconditional love.

She sat down on the bench and lifted the cover to expose keys that were faded and worn from use. She loved pianos like this one, the kind that had been played for so many years, by so many people.

She touched the keys, but she didn't play. Instead, she waited for the fear, the panic. With her eyes closed, she remembered what it felt like to be onstage and be consumed by that fear. But the fear hadn't been about the piano, it had been about the audience watching her. The fear had been about what they would think of her performance.

When the fear didn't grab hold she started to play. "Jesus Loves Me." The words were so simple, the melody was sweet. Jesus loves me, this I know, for the Bible tells me so.

Jesus loves me. Here, in this town, with her grandmother and these people, that love was natural. They all accepted it, as if it were a given. But how did she accept that He could love her that way?

Love her. She tried to remember feeling loved. And the only moment that came to mind was a picnic by a lake and a cowboy. That wasn't love, though. That was…

She didn't know what it was. It was more than her limited experience with life could really fathom. The one thing she knew for sure, it was a memory she would hold on to forever.

After walking the kids from his afternoon group back to the dining hall, where they met up with their counselor, Jason headed down the hill toward the chapel. He couldn't seem to convince himself to let it go.

He heard the piano before he got there. The

tune was simple, "Jesus Loves Me," but it was sweet. Of course it was Alyson. He had watched her walking down there thirty minutes earlier.

He walked up the back steps and stood in the open doorway. She was sitting in front of the piano, playing with one finger, her eyes closed.

While she played, he stayed at the back of the chapel and watched. When she didn't notice him, he sat on the back pew and waited. Her hand came up and she wiped at her cheek.

He should go. Common sense told him that. There were a million things he could be doing. He had kids who wanted to learn to rope. He had cattle of his own that needed to be taken care of.

And instead of doing those things, he sat there, waiting, in case she needed him.

What made her cry? "Jesus Loves Me"? Or playing the piano. Maybe both?

She stopped playing but she stayed on the bench, her head bowed over the keys. He stood, not sure which door to exit from, or how to get away from her.

A sane man would have left, would have ignored her tears, would have called Jenna to talk to her. Calling Jenna was about the only thought he'd had that made sense.

He couldn't remember what he was doing half the time, and he had never been accused of making all the right choices. With her shoulders shaking gently, he moved forward, because he couldn't leave her there alone. And he didn't want anyone else at her side during this moment.

For a guy who knew when to exit a situation, he seemed to have lost all sense of timing.

When he sat down beside her, she did the unexpected; she turned into his arms. He sat there for a few seconds, unsure, and then he wrapped his arms around her and held her as she cried. He tried to tell her it would be okay. He whispered the words through emotion that settled in his throat, and he rocked, back and forth with her in his arms, waiting for her to tell him what she needed.

Strong arms wrapped around her and Alyson had never felt so safe. Jason held her against his solid chest, rocking her gently, his lips brushing against her temple as he whispered that everything would be okay.

After a few minutes, she pulled back and she knew that she had to be a mess, with tear-stained cheeks and swollen eyes. Her nose was probably red. She never looked good when she cried.

Jason smiled and then he wiped her eyes with his hand.

"Should I ask what's wrong, or just give you a shoulder to lean on?" His words melted her eyes into another round of tears. She brushed them away and leaned, resting her forehead on a shoulder that was strong.

"I guess that's your answer," he whispered.

She moved out of his embrace, even though staying would have been good. But that was the problem. If she stayed in his arms, she would want to stay in his life. And how did she do that?

A breeze picked up, and she closed her eyes. How did she explain a lack of faith to a man who had grown up here, surrounded by faith? How did she explain that her life had never been like his? For every moment that his father wasn't invested in his life, Alyson's mother was consumed with hers.

"You were playing the piano." He encouraged, nudging her with his shoulder as they sat side by side on the bench.

She touched the keys again. "Yeah, 'Jesus Loves Me.'"

"It's a good song."

"Is it a song, or does it mean more? 'Jesus loves me, this I know, for the Bible tells me so.' I don't know, Jason. I sat there this morning listening to the chapel service for the children, to a story so simple, and I've never heard it before. I've never heard these stories, about Jesus. Greater love hath no man than this, that he would lay down his life for a friend."

"For you."

She looked up, still conscious that her eyes would be swollen and her nose red. "Excuse me?"

"For you. He laid down his life for you. If you were the only person who ever accepted. If everyone else said a collective 'No, thank you,' He still would have done it. For you."

"It's like accepting that the world is round after years of being told it is flat. How does a person change everything she's ever known or believed?"

"Baby steps. You start by opening the door to faith, and you let that faith grow. You take steps. You test it. It tests you. And you change. Your ideas about God change."

"You make it sound easy, maybe because you've always lived here, always heard the stories. But my world is so far from here. My world…was flat until today."

She couldn't explain it any other way. Her mother. The anger her mother had with the people here, with their beliefs, with their faith. How did Alyson reconcile those two worlds?

"I can't imagine myself in this world, with

this faith. I don't know how to be this person."
She played the song again. "Jesus Loves Me."
"Why would He love me?"

"Because He created you."

She was trying to reconcile that morning's
sermon, about a God who loves uncondition-
ally with a mother whose love always seemed
to have conditions.

Her lawyer had told her to walk away, to find
a new manager and break that connection with
her parents that gave them control of her career.
And she hadn't known how, because she'd
known what it meant to them, to her sisters, and
to the other performers connected to them.

If it had been about her—her alone—it
would have been easy.

She closed the lid down over the piano keys.
Gift. It wasn't a gift; it was a curse. It was
always having to be what other people thought
she should be. It was performing because
people expected it of her, even when she hated
it. It was the stares, the lack of friends and relationships, because people didn't understand.
They didn't get that she was just a person who
played the piano.

"Have you always had faith?" She looked
up, into his brown eyes that were deep with
compassion, and she was moved in new direc-

tions that her heart didn't know how to react to, how to soak up.

"Not always. My mom had faith, enough for all of us, I guess. And then, when she was gone…"

He faltered and looked away, and she knew this was another part of him she was getting to know, the part that hadn't dealt with the death of his mother. This was a man who found it easy to comfort, to joke, but not easy to deal with his own loss and his own pain.

Or at least she thought that was who he was.

"I've had to work through a lot in order to get over being angry with God for taking her."

"Are you still angry?"

He looked away, to the back of the chapel, to a simple wooden cross hanging on the wall.

"No, I'm not." He took hold of her hands, cupping them in his as he lifted them to brush a kiss over her knuckles. "Are you?"

She didn't know how to answer. "I'm not as angry as I was. But it isn't easy, to let go of what my mother did. And then, in April, my sister eloped with my fiancé. Which I can now say I'm glad about, but…"

He blinked a few times. "Bad month, April."

"A little." She managed a smile. "But each day since has gotten better."

"Alyson, can I pray with you?" He still held her hands in his. His thumbs stroked her fingers. He had straddled the bench and was watching her, waiting. And she didn't know what to say, because this time it wasn't frozen pizza they were praying for. This time they were praying for her to find faith.

She nodded and emotion, so heavy it hurt to breathe, settled in her chest. "Please."

They bowed their heads. Ceiling fans hanging from the rafters swished the air downward, circulating but not really cooling. The chapel wasn't fancy. The piano was old and out of tune. The hymnals were held together with tape. But the moment was one that settled in Alyson's heart.

It all became real in that moment.

After he prayed, Jason touched her back and stood up. She remained on the bench, unsure of her next move. What did a person do after praying for faith? How did they meet the next moments of their life? It changed everything. It changed her heart. It changed how she looked at her future. Because she had faith.

"I want you to make sure that Etta knows that we prayed. This is the open door, Alyson. It's a starting point for change. Believe in yourself, in who God created you to be."

She nodded. "Jason, are you going to remember?"

He grinned and winked. "You bet. Even if I have to write it down. Today, Alyson found faith. I think that's something to remember."

Why was he leaving? She stood, wanting to ask that question, but afraid of the answer. She touched his hand and he met her gaze.

"Why are you walking away?"

He paused and she could see in his eyes that he didn't have an answer. "I don't know. Habit, I guess. Will you be okay?"

Walking away was a habit. She filed that away in her memory, so she wouldn't forget, so she wouldn't let it hurt her. Andie had warned her.

She nodded, and then she stood there as he left. She couldn't follow him. She wouldn't be the woman that ran after a man who didn't want to be caught.

Jason made his way to the dining hall, and he'd never been so glad to get anywhere. He sat down at one of the picnic-style tables and put his foot up on the bench of the table across from him. He liked what they'd done with this room. It was decorated with photographs of the kids from the previous year.

Jenna left the kitchen and joined him.

"What's up with you?" She handed him a bottle of water.

"What do you mean, what's up?"

"You know, this memory thing is a problem, but I think that you remember what's going on and you know what I'm talking about. You look terrible."

"Thanks. I think my kneecap is no longer attached to my leg, the ligaments and tendons are slapping around loose, and you want to have a counseling session?"

"Yeah, that's rough."

He felt like an idiot. "I'm sorry, Jen."

"It's okay." She slapped her prosthetic leg. "I'm doing really well. And having a baby. Could life be better?"

"No, I don't think it could. You deserve this."

He remembered back, to Jenna when she was sixteen and afraid. The two of them used to sit together at night, talking about life, about how to make it. They'd never been in love. They'd been friends. She had been the person he talked to, and he was the person she'd turned to when she got into trouble.

"You deserve to be happy, too." She looked at him, not smiling. "I saw you in the chapel with Alyson."

"Great."

"She's pretty terrific. I mean, she has a lot to learn about living here, but she has potential."

"You like her?"

"What I think doesn't matter. You, on the other hand, are going to be working with her."

"Yeah, I've been told. Or warned. But really, she can't ride and she doesn't know a thing about rodeos. I'm sure she'd rather stay in here, in the air-conditioning."

"You think that about me?" Not Jenna's voice. Jason turned and Alyson was standing in the back doorway. Which was why he hadn't seen her come into the dining hall. "Are you the same guy who was in the chapel with me?"

Was Jenna humming, "Goin' to the Chapel"? He thought she might have hummed it as she walked away.

"Yes, I'm the same guy. I'm sorry, Alyson. But the kitchen is great. It's cool and clean. The stables are hot and dusty."

She sat down across from him. "I want to work in the stable."

"Okay, you want the stables. I can handle that." What he really wanted was to head out the door and escape the look in those blue eyes. Angry women, not his thing.

A woman he'd led to faith in God.

The reminder jerked him up by the scruff of the neck. It felt like a huge connection between them, and he didn't want her angry. He wanted her...

In his arms.

The door opened and Jason looked up as Adam Mackenzie entered the building, looking like a big thunderstorm about to hit. The other man's face was a little red and his eyes showed his fury.

"That accountant stole our money!" Adam slammed a notebook down on one of the tables.

Jenna came back from the kitchen, her face pale. She leaned against the stainless-steel counter and waited. They all waited as Adam worked on getting a grip on his temper.

"What does that mean?" Jenna was the first to ask.

"The donations to the camp are gone, and so is Joseph Brooks. I think he left a few thousand dollars in the camp account. Nice of him, huh?"

"Have you called the police?" Jason turned to straddle the bench seat of the cafeteria table so he could face Adam.

"I just called. They're coming out. We're going to try and chase him down, but I have a feeling he and our money are long gone. I should have paid more attention." Adam brushed a hand through his hair and shook his head. He sat down at the table. Jenna walked up behind her husband and put her hands on his shoulders.

"We'll work something out." She leaned in and kissed his cheek.

"Work something out? We have kids here. We have more kids coming in two weeks. How do we work this out?" He shook his head. "I'll transfer money from our private account. We aren't going to let the camp go down."

"You could have a fund-raiser."

They all turned to look at Alyson, whose suggestion had come out of the blue. She was standing a short distance away, and she shrugged. "I'm sorry, I know it isn't any of my business, but that's what I know—charity events."

"I'm afraid all of our supporters are going to take their money elsewhere when they find out what I allowed to happen." Adam shook his head. "I can't believe I didn't catch it sooner. He handed me checks, showed me the books."

"How did you find out?" Jenna asked, as she sat down next to Adam.

"I wrote a check to pay the electric bill and the bank called. The weekly deposit wasn't made."

"Man, I'm really sorry." Jason could write a check. He could help them out. But he knew that his help wouldn't be enough, not when the camp was hosting six groups each summer and then weekend groups in the spring and fall.

"Nothing we can do about it. We'll just have to start over."

"A charity event would work. We could invite people from Tulsa and from this area." Jason smiled at Alyson. "We could headline a pianist from the East Coast and have the kids at camp serve dinner to those who attend. Nothing fancy, maybe spaghetti?"

"I can't…" Alyson shook her head, her eyes watery. "I mean, I don't think it would be a draw. People here don't know me."

"You're still a gifted pianist." Jason didn't get it. Hadn't she offered? He retraced the memory, and he wasn't sure.

"I can't."

"We could have the fund-raiser during the next camp, at the end of June." Jenna suggested, smiling at Alyson.

Jason let it go. And he let Alyson go. She smiled his way as she said her goodbyes. Etta was standing in the yard, waiting for her.

* * *

"The accountant emptied the accounts for Camp Hope." Alyson filled Etta and Andie in on the story as Andie cooked burgers on the grill.

"Do they know where the guy is?" Andie turned, her apron a cow with its tongue hanging out. She slipped the spatula into the tongue that was also a pocket.

"Not a clue." Alyson swirled her glass of iced tea. "I suggested they do a fund-raiser, some kind of charity event. They could incorporate the camp rodeo at the end of June, mixed in with the children performing songs or skits, maybe serve dinner."

"That's a great idea." Etta nodded her approval. "I could contribute a few things to sell or auction.

"In less than a month." Andie shook her head. "The two of you think you could pull that off in that short a time?"

"You could help, instead of telling us we can't manage to do it," Etta scolded. "And don't let the burgers burn."

"I can't believe we're having veggie burgers." Andie shook her head. "We live in Oklahoma. It should be a law that we only eat beef."

Alyson smiled, because this was family.

"What about you, Ms. La-Di-Dah?" Andie

pointed the spatula her direction. "Are you going to perform?"

Then it wasn't amusing. "No, but I could help get it all organized. I have a lot of experience with events like this."

"Because you've performed in them?" Andie kept it going.

"I can't do it." Alyson stared at her sister. Andie glared back.

"Come clean, Sis. Tell us why you can't."

"Because I have panic attacks when I walk on stage." Alyson picked up her kitten to keep it from clawing its way up her pant leg. "Because until I came here I was on medication for anxiety. And I can't go back to being that person."

"So face your fears." Andie tossed it out, as if it would be that simple. "Figure out what you're afraid of. It can't be the piano."

"No, it isn't the piano." Alyson looked to her grandmother for support. On the ride home they had talked about faith, about trusting God. So how did she put that into action?

How did she become a person who trusted? Jason had said baby steps. A baby step was helping with a charity event. She could help the children with their talents.

She wasn't ready to get back on stage in front of people.

"Let's talk about this later." Etta pointed to the grill. "I think what you need to think about is how to keep those burgers from burning."

"And how to make them edible," Andie muttered as she flipped their dinner off the grill onto a plate.

Alyson smiled a "thank you" at her grandmother. But she knew the conversation wasn't over. This was a conversation she needed to have with herself, about facing her fears.

Eventually she would have to go back to her life as Alyson Anderson. She would have to go back to Boston, back on stage.

On Friday Alyson walked down to the stables of Camp Hope. Her first day working there. Jason wasn't around yet. She didn't mind. She loved the peacefulness and the quiet of the stable. It was a new discovery—her love for dusty barns, the sweaty smell of horses and the sweet scent of hay.

As she walked through the double doors, a horse whinnied a greeting. Alyson took that as an invitation. She stopped at the stall and the horse's head came over the top of the gate, rubbing against her arm. The gray with his dappled coat was one of her favorites.

"Have you ever been afraid?" She smiled

as she rubbed the horse's ears. "Of course you haven't."

"Why are you afraid?" A voice asked from the open doorway of the stable. "Are you talking to the horse about the fund-raiser?"

Jason. She turned and then avoided him by letting the horse nip at her sleeve. She ran a hand down the soft, gray neck and breathed in the scent of horse.

"I am, and he's a good listener. It's hard to explain." She glanced over her shoulder at him. "It just happens."

"Alyson, it was your idea, the fund-raiser. Or did I miss something?"

"You didn't miss anything. A fund-raiser is always good. The kids can have the spaghetti dinner. I bet there are kids here who have talent. If they sing or play, we can showcase their talents. You can add the showdeo. It could be a great thing for the camp. We don't charge. We ask for donations to the camp."

"Right. It is a great idea. And yet, you ran the minute I mentioned your involvement."

"I can't play."

"Of course you can. I've heard you play."

She turned away from the horse and faced a man who was asking her about the things she kept hidden deep inside, out of the spotlight.

"*I can't play.*" It was easier to say it, after having told Andie and Etta. "I walked off the stage a few weeks ago. I can't play."

Jason took his hat off and hung it on a hook nearby. He leaned against the wall, waiting. "Why did you walk off the stage?"

"I can't play on a stage without falling apart." She walked to the doors of the barn and he joined her. He was still limping and he leaned against the door, watching her. "I have panic attacks. When I left Boston I decided to end a ten-year relationship with medication for those attacks. I've only taken the pills because that's how I walk onstage. That's how I face a crowd." It was how she faced herself.

And now he knew the truth.

"It's okay to be afraid."

"It isn't okay when fear keeps you from doing what you have to do."

She looked out at the field, and then at the sky. There were clouds in the distance. Dark gray and eating up the blue sky as they moved north.

"Looks like a storm coming." Jason followed her gaze. "Think we ought to head back?"

She shook her head. She wasn't ready to head back. From where she stood, she could see the children with their group leaders. They had classes after breakfast and then craft time.

"Jason, I'll help plan the fund-raiser. I'll help the children in any way that I can. I'm not sure if I can play."

His arm slid around her waist and she wondered how his touch made her feel stronger, almost made her believe she could walk on stage and conquer her fear.

"No one is going to push you to do something you're not ready to do. I'm sorry if you felt like I was pushing. I didn't realize." His voice was low, husky and tinged with an Oklahoma accent that softened it all, making it easy to hear.

She turned to look up at him, at a cowboy with a Robert Redford smile and brown eyes so warm, so kind, she wanted to…to touch him. How had that happened, that twenty-eight years of holding back ended with this moment of wanting to let go and feel a little of what everyone else felt, even their pain? Even if it meant being afraid.

His pain. She sometimes saw flashes of it in the depths of his eyes. But he always wiped it away with a smile and a joke.

"George Strait," he whispered.

"What?"

"On the radio." He held her hand in his and his left hand went to her waist.

She paused, barely hearing the song that

filtered from somewhere farther down in the stable. He held her close and they swayed to the music and then he twirled her in a circle under his arm and pulled her close again.

She reached up, touching his cheek, resting her palm there. His head bent and she waited, breathless in a way that was full of wonder and a fear that didn't create panic, but made her wait, expecting something beautiful.

The horse nuzzled her arm as she leaned back against the stall door, Jason in front of her, his eyes tender and warm, holding her captive.

His lips touched hers and she leaned into him. His hands cupped her cheeks as he made her breathless.

"Alyson, you are so beautiful," he said softly, holding her close as he kissed her again.

He made her feel beautiful, and strong.

When the kiss ended, she held him close as they returned to a world that was crashing with thunder, sweeping a breeze through the stable and kicking up dust in the field.

"Wow, did we do that?" He laughed a little shakily as he leaned on the door of the stall next to her, holding her with an arm wrapped around her waist.

"I think we must have." Her voice trembled and she wanted to sit down.

Outside lightning flashed across the sky, followed by a crash of thunder. She jumped a little.

"Come on, let's go down to the office and drag out a couple of chairs. We can't go anywhere until this is over, we might as well have a cup of coffee and enjoy watching it rain."

The two of them, alone, while her emotions were doing cartwheels and her brain was trying to drag her back to reality. Her brain and her emotions were clashing, creating a storm of their own that she knew she couldn't outrun.

In the beginning she had allowed herself to believe that it was the newness of being here, of knowing someone like Jason, that created the intensity of her emotions. But the more she knew him, the more she wanted to be near him.

She watched from the door of the office as Jason filled the coffeepot with water from the watercooler and then scooped coffee into the filter basket. He switched it on and then reached for a couple of folded canvas chairs.

He handed her the chairs and sidestepped out of the office, holding the doorframe as he eased down. He smiled at her, winking as he took the chairs back.

"I'm not getting any younger." He said it with a lightness that she had to wonder about.

Did it really not bother him? Was he really capable of joking about an injury that could possibly rob him of his career?

Or was she right, and that's how he handled life? He made a joke of the things he didn't want to deal with, to smooth over his pain.

"It can't be that easy." She took one of the chairs and unfolded it in the doorway of the stable, back far enough to keep them out of the wind and rain, close enough to feel the cool breeze.

He sat down next to her. "I'm getting my memory back. My knee is probably going to need surgery, but it'll get better."

"I don't know if anyone is that strong." She didn't look at him. Instead, she watched the rolling clouds of the storm sweep across the vast openness that was Oklahoma. "I hope there aren't any tornadoes."

Gray skies and green grass met at the horizon line. The temperature cooled and Alyson shivered.

"Someone would come get us, or call my cell phone if there were." Jason reached for her hand. "Relax."

She sat for a moment, his hand strong and firm on hers. She listened to the coffeepot as it gurgled and then was silent.

"I'll get our coffee."

"Thanks." Jason touched her arm before she could walk away. "And you're right. It isn't always easy."

Chapter Nine

Jason drove up to the camp the morning after the storm had blown through, taking shingles off one of the dorms and knocking limbs from a few trees. And in a sense, doing things to his heart he hadn't expected. But that had been a storm of a different kind. That storm had happened inside the stable and it was still pounding at him, making him relive a moment when he'd held Alyson in his arms and he had realized something about himself.

He had realized that for the first time in years he was being honest with his emotions and the woman he had held shifted that for him, making him reach out instead of tucking it all inside. For a guy who rode bulls for a living, he had thrived on safe. Safe relationships.

Because as far back as he could remember,

only a few people lasted. He had a few guys on the bull-riding circuit that were still friends. But being in that life, traveling from event to event, things were always changing. People came and went.

You got used to guys leaving due to injuries, or because they got bumped to the lower event levels. Some got married and gave it up.

And Jason had lived that life, traveling, dating the women he met on the road, and never really staying in anyone's life long enough to get attached.

He hadn't minded at all. It had suited him.

A storm had changed that for him. A storm had pushed him further into the arms of a woman than he'd ever been. Because there had been a moment when he held her that he couldn't imagine ever letting go.

He parked his truck in the grassy field that was the parking lot for Camp Hope. He sat for a minute, relieved that he could remember yesterday. And then wishing he could forget.

But he hadn't been able to forget her since she first arrived. Cashmere and lavender. How in the world had those two things led to his downfall? He'd never been the kind of guy to fall for cashmere. His women had worn jeans and knew how to rope a calf, brand a steer and drive a four-wheel drive truck through mud, with a stock trailer on the back.

Alyson had traded her cashmere for blue jeans and T-shirts.

He climbed out of his truck and headed up the driveway to the stable. It was early and the campers were starting to stir, but the place was still pretty quiet.

If he had time this morning, he wanted to do a little roping with one of the new horses that Adam had bought, just to make sure it was gentle enough for a novice rider.

He walked through the stable to the gated entry at the end. The horse in question, a big chestnut, burnished red and with a wide, white blaze running down his face was in the corral waiting. The animal trotted to the gate.

Jason snapped a lead rope onto the halter and led the horse through the gate, latching it closed behind them.

"Time for us to see what you can do."

"He's pretty gentle."

Jason turned and nodded at Adam. "Yeah, I think he'll be fine. There's a boy with a little riding experience. I'm going to teach him to rope and see what the two of them can do."

"Jenna talked to Alyson and she thinks we should plan the charity dinner and concert for the same day as the showdeo at the end of the next two week camp. That would be short notice, just three weeks, but it would bring in quite a few people."

Jason cross-tied the horse in the center aisle of the stable. He walked through the door into the tack room and flipped on the light. There were a dozen or more saddles, bridles and other tack, brushes, and buckets neatly stored inside the room. It smelled like leather and bug spray.

He walked back out with the bridle and saddle. "That would be good. I've already been making calls. But Adam, I don't know if Alyson can do this. She's willing to help with the planning, but she might not be up to the concert part."

"Why do you say that?"

"Just leave it up to her." Jason slid the saddle pad into place on the horse's back, then the saddle. The gelding twitched a little, stomped at a fly on his leg and then settled. Jason tightened the girth strap.

"Whatever you say." Adam gave him another look, and Jason ignored the grin on the other man's face.

"Yeah, whatever I say. Turn a calf loose in the arena."

The horse walked next to him, as if it had

been his horse for years and knew exactly what was expected of him. The previous owners had said the horse had been used in small rodeos, but a guy never knew for sure.

The sun was burning the last of the dew off the grass and heating up the morning as Jason slid his foot into the stirrup and lifted himself into the saddle. His right leg went over the horse's back and he settled into the seat.

"Easy there, boy." Jason held the reins and waited for the gelding to settle. He could feel the shifting, feel the horse tense. "You aren't going to throw me, big guy."

The horse moved a few steps, stomping and then nodding his head a little as he fought the bit.

"Don't tell me I got ripped again." Adam stood outside the arena, leaning on the gate.

"No, he's just restless. And I think he's afraid of the calf." What kind of roping horse was afraid of a calf?

Like a pianist afraid to play the piano. It could happen.

Jason pulled back on the reins and the horse backed at his command. "Not bad."

He rested the reins on the animal's neck and put pressure on his left side. The horse turned to the right. Jason nodded and touched his heels into the horse's side. With that silent command the gelding broke into a slow trot. They circled the arena and the calf stayed ahead of them. When Jason was ready and thought the horse was ready he gave another light nudge and the animal broke into an easy lope, inside front leg leading, head down at a nice level. He adjusted, pulling back on the reins, and the horse walked.

Jason rode back to the gate. "He'll make a good pleasure class horse. Put a kid on him for that and he'll be fine. I'll try using him for roping, but if he's a Western pleasure horse, that's where I'd keep him."

The horse was meant to show, not rodeo. He had the gait, didn't have to be encouraged to lead off on the right leg. It was a no-brainer as far as Jason was concerned. He swung his leg over the saddle and dismounted.

He landed with a jolt that jarred his leg and he took in a quick breath. "Wow, that wasn't good."

"When are you going to have that surgery?" Adam opened the gate and Jason led the horse out.

"One of these days." He stopped while Adam latched the gate. Out of the corner of his eye he saw movement. Alyson and the boy who wanted to learn to rope. He had really thought the chestnut gelding would be a great fit. Back to the drawing board on that.

"Alyson, Trent, you guys are down here early."

Alyson shrugged a little and looked away, her cheeks flushed pink. "I work down here, remember?"

Oh yeah. She worked down here. And she was dressed for the occasion in clothes that looked right off the rack and boots that were still a little too shiny. She'd have blisters tonight and tomorrow she wouldn't be smiling. He'd seen a pair of boots in the tack room. If he could talk her into wearing those, she'd be a lot happier. Or at least more comfortable.

"You want to try this horse out, Trent?" Jason held the reins of the saddled chestnut and waited for the boy to stop looking overwhelmed.

The kid, lanky and with hair the color of straw, finally shrugged. Man, Jason remembered that age. About thirteen, when everything felt awkward and there was a new experience every day, making a guy feel like he might never understand life or girls.

Especially one like Alyson, who didn't give it all away with a smile and a look in her eyes. She kept a part of herself back and left something for a guy to discover.

He thought he might have to kiss her again

later, just to get her to let go of that dangerous look she was wearing.

"I'd like to ride him." Trent finally found command of the English language, and then his face turned red and he looked down at the ground.

Jason got it then, the kid was in love with Alyson. Well, a guy couldn't blame him for that.

"Come on then, let's walk you into the arena and you can show me what you know. Now the thing about this horse is, I don't think he's a roping horse. He's more of a show horse. But we'll work on roping later."

"Thank you, sir." The boy followed Jason through the open gate. When Jason held the headstall of the bridle, the kid put his foot in the stirrup and then half climbed into the saddle.

The gelding twitched a little but he didn't out and out throw the kid. Trent thunked himself into the saddle and moved his legs a little too much in the stirrups. The horse still didn't move.

"First off, let's keep the movements to a minimum." Jason put the reins in Trent's hands.

"Yes, sir."

"Take it easy to start with. You know the basic commands from our lesson yesterday. So take him around the arena. One lap at a walk, once at a trot and then an easy lope. Don't let him take control."

The boy nodded and turned the horse away from the group of adults who were watching. As he rode away, they all seemed to let out a collective sigh of relief. Jason stayed inside the arena, just in case.

"Any news on the accountant?" He didn't turn to look at Adam, but kept his attention on the boy and the horse. They were still walking, plodding along. The boy held the reins correctly and rode with his back straight.

"They've got a few leads, but the money has been disappearing for months. I guess I never thought someone would embezzle from a camp for kids. And he was smart about it. The books looked clean. It seemed that everything was getting paid. But the biggest loss was through donations. Money that came in and never made it to our account."

"I'm really sorry." Jason nodded to the boy as he rode past. "Loosen up on the reins. That's the reason he's shaking his head."

The boy nodded and kept riding, but his hands moved a little and the horse settled into a trot, the head bobbing stopped.

"This too shall pass." Adam shrugged. "I was ready to go after the guy, but Jenna, man, she's all faith. She's positive God will take what this guy meant for bad and use it for good for us."

Alyson was shaking her head. "How can this be good? How can God let this happen to a camp that only does good things?"

Adam looked at Jason and Jason didn't know what to say. He knew she needed an answer, because he knew her. He knew her life.

"Life happens, Alyson. People do things that we don't get. People hurt us. But we find faith." He shook his head. "That sounds like an easy answer, but it's the only one that I have. You pray. You find a way to forgive. You trust God to redeem the situation. And through it all, our faith grows. We get stronger."

"Forgive." She looked away, blue eyes the color of the blue sky and blond hair lifting in the light breeze. "That's the part that isn't easy."

"No, it isn't."

Jason reached to touch her shoulder, but he stopped himself.

Adam had walked away, into the barn, leaving them alone. Not too subtle, Jason thought. He turned his attention back to the horse and its young rider. The animal was in an easy canter, smooth and controlled. The rider looked a little less than confidant and kind of bouncy.

"Tighten up your legs and settle into the saddle," Jason called out. The boy nodded, just a little and Jason could see that he was trying.

The horse and rider came around the arena again and slowed to a stop in front of Adam. "Move with the horse. Find his rhythm and let that be your rhythm in the saddle. I know it sounds easy, but the more you focus on that, the easier this will be."

"Got it." Trent took in a deep breath, as if he could suck in confidence with oxygen. And maybe he could. Jason nodded in the direction of the arena.

"One more time. Walk once, canter once and bring him in."

"I told Jenna that I could make phone calls. I do know people who could help with the concert." Alyson spoke as the boy rode away. "I want to help."

"I know you do." Jason opened the gate and walked out of the arena. "Listen, don't feel like you have to do this, Alyson. People will understand. Besides, the other help you can give will mean a lot."

"Right." She shot a glance past him, at the arena and Trent. "He's in trouble."

Jason turned back just as the horse started to sidestep and then arch his back and buck.

"Trent, hold tight with your knees. Don't let him throw you off. Keep his head up."

The horse bucked a few more times. The boy went forward in the saddle, but landed back in the seat. He kept his knees tight.

"Keep a firm hold and turn his head back this way. Distract him from wanting to buck." Sometimes that worked.

Trent followed every command and when they turned back, the horse broke into a stiff-legged walk, but obeyed his rider. Trent shook like a leaf on one of the maple trees during a good wind.

"Buddy, you stayed on him."

"I heard a bee." Trent looked a little pale and his voice trembled. "I think he got stung or something in the ear. His ears were really twitching."

Jason walked back through the gate. "Okay, come here, Red."

He took the bridle and nodded for the boy to dismount. When Trent was on the ground, Jason checked the horse over. Sure enough, he had a red mark in his ear where something had stung him.

"You did good, Trent. I'm proud of you. A horse like Red needs a rider like you, one who isn't going to panic. Tomorrow we'll work on roping. I think he might be willing to do double duty for you."

Trent's face lit up. "You think?"

"I think." Jason handed the reins over to the teen. "Take him inside. Cross-tie him and take his saddle off. He'll need a good brushing and some grain before you put him out in the field."

"Yes, sir." Trent led the horse away, his back a little straighter.

That's why Jason was at Camp Hope. Moments like this made it all clear. It made sense, working with these kids, making their lives a little better, giving them a little more confidence. It hooked him, and how did a guy walk away from that?

How did he go back on the road, to airplanes, motels and a different city or town every weekend? How did Jason go back to his life?

And women. None of them knew him. They knew that he was a bull rider. They loved the excitement at an event. They wore little tops, tight jeans and polished boots, but they didn't care about him, about his life.

Some of that was his fault. He'd never really cared to share his life with any of them.

Alyson walked next to him, back to the barn. Sometimes she felt like a complication. Sometimes she felt like the best thing that had ever happened to him. He shook his head, because never in a million years would he have dreamed up this scenario.

But God had. Jason wouldn't have been home when she showed up if it hadn't been for the accident. He nearly stopped walking when that thought shifted through his mind.

"You're good with these kids." Alyson pulled him back to a hot summer day and her presence next to him.

"I enjoy working with them."

"More than bull riding?"

He glanced down, wondering how she could do that, how she could know what he was thinking. Of course she didn't. It was coincidence.

"I don't know. Bull riding has always been my career. It's been in my blood for a long time."

"Are you going to compete again?"

She was so formal about it. He wanted to laugh, but he didn't. Instead, he led her into the stable and they stood back and watched as Trent took care of his horse.

"I'm scheduled for an event in a month. I'm going to Clint's to get on practice bulls tomorrow morning."

"Is that dangerous?"

"No, not really. Come with me. I'll show you."

As soon as the invitation was out, he knew

that it changed everything. He knew that it made her someone he wouldn't walk away from before it hurt.

Alyson walked past the chapel on her way to the dining hall. Jason was still in the stable, helping a few of the younger children learn to pole bend. She'd watched him set up the poles, spacing them a short distance apart in the arena, making a line that the horses would run through, weaving back and forth through the poles. She didn't quite get it, but he'd promised to let her try it tomorrow.

On a horse. She could ride one around the arena, or through the field. But around poles?

As she passed the chapel, she heard the piano. She glanced in and saw a few of the children gathered around it. They plunked at the keys and managed something that sounded like "Twinkle, Twinkle." Turning off the trail that led to the dining hall, she walked over to the chapel, through the open door at the end.

One of the girls looked up, eyes wide. "We were just playing."

"That's okay, keep playing." Alyson walked down the center aisle between the two rows of pews. There were four girls and two boys, Jenna's twins. She smiled at Timmy and David and they smiled back—big smiles that lit up their smudged faces.

"We were just playing the piano," said a smaller girl. She had curly brown hair and big brown eyes. "I've never played one and Timmy said we could touch this one."

"You can touch it." Alyson walked up behind the group. "Would you like for me to show you how to play?"

They all nodded. David's smile grew. "'Cause she's a professional piani…" He scrunched his nose. "Pianoist."

"Something like that. A pianist." She ran a hand over his blond head. His hair had been buzzed short and his feet were bare. "Where are your shoes?"

"Lost. The dog took 'em."

"Oh." She sat down and the children circled around her. Her heart pounded, but this time it wasn't fear, it was something like being filled up. She smiled and touched the keys, running her fingers over them and getting a thrill that had been missing for a long, long time.

What made it different?

She played a few children's songs, including "Twinkle, Twinkle."

"Don't you need a book?" The little girl with

curly hair had settled on the bench next to Alyson.

"No, I don't. I play by ear." The songs had always been in her head. It was hard for anyone to understand. She could hear a song and know how to play it.

"Can you play the song 'In the Garden.'" The older girl that had originally explained their presence in the chapel moved forward. "I love that song."

"Can you hum it for me?"

The girl, in a sweet alto, sang the song. As she sang, Alyson started to play. The song was beautiful, the melody pure. The words, about walking in the garden with the Savior, reached deep into Alyson's heart, to her soul.

She had a savior. Tears clouded her vision as she played and the young girl sang about Jesus telling her she was His own.

The song ended and the girl leaned and hugged her close. "Are you okay, Miss Alyson?"

"I'm fine, sweetie. You know what I think? I think we should practice a song that you can do this Sunday."

The children nodded. One of the girls suggested a song that they all knew and Alyson listened to excited chatter. As they talked, the bell rang, signaling lunch.

The children scattered. David, one of Jenna's twins, was the last to leave. Before he turned to run after the other kids, he hugged her tight. And then he was gone.

Alyson wiped her tears and took a deep breath. Her fingers moved to the piano keys again. She played the song and this time she sang the words that she remembered.

Jason stood on the trail and listened to the music that drifted from the chapel. Sun beat down on his back and he moved into the shade of a tree and leaned against it for support. The song was "In the Garden." He closed his eyes and listened to a child singing the lyrics. And he knew that it was Alyson playing the piano.

His mother's song. They had even played it at her funeral.

The child's voice faded as the song ended. He stood there, listening to the children talk, and Alyson laughing to something they said. The lunch bell rang and the children ran from the chapel, up the hill to the dining hall. That had been his destination, too. He just hadn't made it.

Before he could step away from the tree, the piano picked up the tune again. This time it was Alyson who sang the words.

He walked down the trail to the chapel. This

was different than the last time, when she had picked out the words to "Jesus Loves Me."

This time she was singing about something personal.

And he knew he should walk away. He had experience with walking out the door, not with staying to feel the pain. He liked his life uncomplicated.

It had been anything but since Alyson showed up at Etta's.

That should scare him, but it didn't.

She stopped playing and looked up, her gaze connecting with his. She closed the piano up and stood, no longer a woman from the city. She had transformed herself into what she wanted to be, a Forester.

Who was she really? He didn't think she had an answer to that question. As much as she wanted this transformation, he had to wonder if it was that easy to shed who she had always been.

"You're missing lunch." He stood at the back of the chapel and she walked down the aisle toward him. The sun peeked through the leaves of shade trees that had been left standing around the chapel. The golden beam found her, catching the blond of her hair in its light.

And Jason felt a tingle of fear, because of

this woman, walking up the aisle of the chapel to join him. He swallowed hard and tried to think of something funny to say, and he couldn't get the words out, couldn't shove them past the lump in his throat.

"I was heading for the dining hall when I heard the children on the piano," she admitted as she got closer to him.

And then they were standing there, at the back of the chapel, and his eyes ached because of sunlight and because she had consumed the air around him.

Man, she obviously didn't get that he had a reputation for not getting trapped in relationships.

"I'll walk up with you," he offered. "You might have to pull me up the hill."

She glanced down, at his swollen knee and she shook her head. "You're a lost cause."

"Not too much." He hooked his arm through hers. "They're having a bonfire for supper tonight."

"I know, hot dogs."

"And s'mores." He leaned a little toward her, because her hair smelled like coconut and her lips sparkled with pink gloss.

"So, will you go with me?" he asked.

She shot him a look. "You're that cheap?

You want me to accept an invitation to a bonfire that I'm already attending?"

He shrugged. "I did promise you a bonfire. This one is already being built and I don't have to do the work."

She looked up at him, smiling. That pink gloss was more temptation than any man could handle.

"That's pretty cheesy."

He pretty much agreed, but he didn't have anything better. He thought he could go for the broken cowboy routine. He'd had experience with that, and it had a way of working on women.

But Alyson was different, and he couldn't play those games with her.

"I'll pick you up at seven?" They were already at the dining hall and kids were filing in.

Alyson nodded a little, and he wasn't even sure if she was agreeing. But he planned on knocking on her door at six-thirty.

Chapter Ten

Andie knocked on the frame of the open door of the bedroom and Alyson turned away from the mirror. Andie stepped into the room. She had a backpack flung over her shoulder and she'd been rushing through the house all afternoon, getting ready to leave.

"I'm outta here." Andie plopped down on the chair next to the window. "And you look like a woman getting ready for a date, not a bonfire at a Christian camp."

"Will you be back next week?" Alyson shifted the conversation, she hoped, to something neutral.

"Probably. Are you going to be here?" Andie propped booted feet on the window seat.

Would she be here? Alyson sat down on the edge of her bed and slipped her feet into flip-flops. "Of course I'll be here. I'm working at the camp. I'm not going to walk away from that."

She had talked to Jenna about working with the children, teaching them a few songs that they could sing. They were thinking of bringing these kids back for the fund-raiser, so they could participate. The kids were begging their own church to let them return.

"Alyson, can I give you a little advice, if it isn't too late?"

"Do I have a choice?"

Andie laughed. "Actually, no, you don't. I was just going to remind you to be careful with your heart, sister."

Jason. Of course that's what Andie meant with that advice.

"My heart is still intact. I've already been dumped and I'm not about to go through that again."

"Yeah, but I don't think you loved that guy."

"No, I probably didn't."

Andie dropped her feet to the ground and stood up. She leaned to kiss Alyson on the top of her head. "See you soon. And I don't want a message on my voice mail telling me you've eloped with a cowboy."

"That isn't going to happen."

As Andie walked out the door, she laughed. "We'll see."

Alyson mumbled that she didn't have to see, she knew. But because of Andie, she found herself thinking about Jason, and a night that felt like a first date.

She thought back, to dating Dan. It hadn't really been dating. He'd taken her to dinner twice a month. That had been their schedule. And each date had ended with a friendly kiss that hadn't shattered anything more than her dreams of what love should feel like.

Now she knew the truth. Dan had been comparing her to her sister, to Laura's more dramatic beauty. Laura had dazzled him with her bright laughter and easy personality.

Alyson hated that she understood. She'd always been slightly dazzled by Laura, too. But she still loved her sister.

A truck rumbled down the road outside Etta's. Alyson listened as it turned into the driveway and pulled up to the house. He hadn't forgotten. She smiled, because she had hoped, just a little, that he might forget.

Instead, he was knocking on the front door and Etta was yelling up the stairs that her date was here. Her date. Alyson was twenty-eight and she felt like she was going to the prom.

It wasn't the prom. It was hot dogs and a bonfire at Camp Hope. She stood up, shot a quick glance at the mirror, and walked out the door. He was waiting at the bottom of the stairs and for a second it felt like the prom. Except that she was in shorts and a T-shirt, he was in jeans, but tonight, no hat. He wore an unbuttoned short-sleeved shirt over a T-shirt.

He smiled up at her, and her heart tumbled down the stairs. She grabbed the rail to make sure she didn't follow and reminded herself that this was one night, and not forever.

"Ready to go?" He winked and she wondered if he had a clue how nervous she was.

"Of course." This was the new, stronger version of herself. Like a new computer program, updated and more sophisticated. Her less confident self reminded her that new programs were always full of bugs and tended to crash often. "Of course I'm ready."

She had reached the bottom of the stairs and he reached for her hand. "You're driving."

"I can't drive a truck." She glanced at Etta. "Tell him this is a bad idea."

"Of course you can. You need the practice." He handed her the keys.

"See you kids later." Etta was pushing them

to the door, like they were sixteen. "Have fun and stop worrying."

And then the door was closing behind them. Jason took hold of her hand and held it tight as they walked to the truck. This had nothing to do with her needing experience driving a stick shift. She considered asking him the real reason, but he was as entitled to his secrets as she was to hers.

He stopped at the driver's side of his truck and opened the door for her. She climbed in, but she didn't let him close the door.

"We could take my car," she offered.

"Nope, not into the field." He closed the door and walked around to the passenger side. "Put your foot on the clutch and the gas, make sure it's in first gear and start your engines."

"No race car analogies, please."

Alyson started the truck, and that proved to be the easy part. Shift, clutch, brake, gas, shift, don't forget the clutch, grinding gears, man next to her mumbling under his breath and then trying to smile. On the highway outside of Dawson it got easier. She could put the truck in fourth gear and drive like a normal person.

"As we get close to the camp entrance, slow down, use the clutch and shift to Third. Then slow again, clutch, shift to Second."

"Okay." But it wasn't okay. Her hands, legs and insides were shaking.

He laughed. "You're doing great."

She shifted once, twice and on the third shift the truck bucked, jerked and died.

"Oops." She shifted into First and started it again.

He leaned back in the seat. "Up the driveway to the barn."

"And then you can take over?"

He shook his head. "You're doing a great job."

The gate was already open. She drove through, afraid she'd hit the truck against the posts on either side. And from the way he sucked in a breath, he had to be thinking the same thing.

In the distance she could see a stand of trees and a group of people. The fire was already burning, smoke swirling into the air and kids standing around it. The truck bounced as she drove across the field toward the group of people who had already gathered.

"Park at the end of the row." Jason pointed. There were several trucks and a tractor attached to a trailer. That was for the hayride they planned to have.

She parked the truck and started to turn the key, but Keith Urban was playing on the radio, and she liked his music. Jason opened his door and got out of the truck.

Alyson left the music on and stepped out. She started to reach in the back for their lawn chairs and the blanket Jason had brought along, but she didn't. Jason stood at the back of the truck, a hand on the tailgate and his head down.

She walked back to him. He opened his eyes and smiled, winking as if nothing had happened.

"You're not okay."

"Of course I am." He slipped an arm around her waist and walked her around the truck to where she'd left the chairs and blanket. Keith Urban was still singing and Jason swayed a little, catching himself on the side of the truck.

She started to comment, but he stopped her with a look.

"I think this song might be my favorite." He moved closer. "What about you?"

A love song, sung in pure Keith Urban style, twirling a woman's emotions. Alyson pretended the song didn't matter, and that this moment with the sun setting behind the dark green of the trees, turning the sky a brilliant orange and pink didn't matter. She was standing in a field with a man whose smile touched deep inside her and she really wanted it to not matter.

But it did.

Nothing had ever mattered more.

As he pulled her close, she no longer felt like a person coming unraveled, losing herself. For that moment, with Keith Urban singing and a cowboy holding her close, she felt the promise of a summer night.

He leaned, kissed her cheek and then whispered in her ear, "We'd better join the group before we forget why we're here."

"For s'mores," she whispered back.

"Exactly."

But she was breathless and his hand lingered on hers for a few seconds more.

Jason carried the chairs and walked next to Alyson, not reaching for her hand as they neared a group of people who wore openly curious expressions. He wasn't going to satisfy their curiosity. And he wasn't going to fall on his face from the bout of dizziness that had hit him about the time he left his house for Etta's to pick up Alyson.

He was waiting for the medication to kick in and praying it wouldn't take long.

He wasn't going to be able to keep making excuses, like telling Alyson she needed to practice driving. And then holding on to her instead of falling.

Alyson opened her chair and then she walked away, drawn to the rope swing the kids were using to swing out over the swimming hole. Some took longer to let go than others. Jason watched, laughing because the girl on the swing had been over the water twice and she was still hanging tight. Adam and Jenna were standing nearby, encouraging her to let go.

Let go. Jason shot a glance in Alyson's direction. She knew about letting go. When he'd held her in his arms, she had let go. He'd seen it in her eyes, that she was beginning to see who she was. She was Alyson Forester, from Dawson.

She was good at being that Alyson.

Not that he minded the Alyson who wore cashmere.

She probably wanted that cashmere right now, he thought. It wasn't cold, but she hugged herself as if she were chilled. He thought about offering the jacket he kept behind the seat of his truck, but knew she wouldn't take it. She wasn't cold, just trying to pull herself together.

He understood.

He could barely remember the first day he met her, but he knew that the shreds of memory he had retained meant something. He couldn't let go of seeing her standing at the edge of Etta's lawn, staring at him, at that big house, as if she'd just entered another dimension.

Or found something she'd lost.

And maybe she had lost something— herself. But he thought she was finding that person again. He also thought that when she found herself, she'd leave. Once her confidence was back and her life wasn't about fearing her gift, or fearing rejection, she'd return to the life she'd left behind.

He walked to the edge of the creek bank where she was standing. She glanced at him and then back up, at the rope swing.

"You should try it," he suggested, and she shook her head.

"I don't think I'm dressed for plunging into a creek." She watched as the next teenager took the rope, walked back and then glided forward, swinging over the water. This kid dropped on the first try. "Is it deep?"

"It's over their heads."

"I'd like to come back and try it. Someday." She sighed and didn't look at him. "Before I leave."

"Are you planning to leave?" Why did that question land somewhere in his gut?

"Eventually." She was still watching the kids

on the rope. "I have a schedule that I can't walk away from."

"Yeah, I get that."

This time she looked at him, her blue eyes bright. "I knew this was temporary."

He nodded, because he'd known it, too. She should be easy to let go of. He'd go back on the road, back to riding bulls. She'd go back to her world.

Jenna called out for the kids, telling them it was time to eat. They walked out of the creek and hurried back to the fire, flinging towels around their shoulders. Alyson reached for his hand.

"Stop pretending." She spoke so softly he barely caught it.

"What?"

"You, acting like you're okay, like you just wanted to let me practice driving a stick shift."

He smiled and winked, because he didn't know what to say to someone who saw way too much.

"How do you like your hot dogs?" he asked as they got closer to the fire, to the group of people already shoving hot dogs on sticks. A few were standing close to the fire with sticks held close to the flames.

"Well, since I've never had one roasted on a

fire, I'll let you help me with that. And I asked you a question."

He laughed. "I never thought you'd be this stubborn."

"You don't know me very well."

He looked at her, at a woman with a soft smile and blue eyes that held his attention. He knew her better than he had planned on knowing her.

"Then I guess I'll have to get to know you better." He moved a little closer and she stepped back, her eyes bright with laughter and her hair coming loose from the clip that held it in place.

She was definitely determined to get under his skin.

"Not so fast, Cowboy." She was still teasing, still smiling. "I have questions."

He shrugged. "Yes, I really am naturally this charming and cute."

"Oh, so you really are one of those love 'em and leave 'em types?"

He laughed. "Yeah, honey, that's me."

And it had been, for a long time.

"Funny, but I don't see you that way." Her smile dissolved and her eyes studied him, holding his gaze until he felt fifteen and unsure.

"How do you see me?" This wasn't working

out the way he had planned, as a way to distract her.

He wasn't sure he wanted to know how she saw him. And really didn't want this conversation to take place with an audience. He smiled across the fire, at Willow and Clint, holding the little girl they'd adopted from China.

"I see you as a guy who is always laughing and smiling so he doesn't have to deal with how much he hurts on the inside."

"I think we should roast hot dogs."

"Exactly my point." And she took her roasting stick and walked away, leaving him as unsure as he'd ever been in his life.

From across the fire he saw Clint Cameron laugh and sign something to his wife. They were looking at him. Willow signed back and Clint nodded.

Married couples. They thought everyone should follow their example.

Alyson had joined Jenna on the lawn chairs a short distance from the fire. He thought about joining them, but instead he went the opposite direction, finding a place with a group of teenage boys who were intent on discussing the steer riding they would do the next day.

That was a lot safer than any other conversation Jason thought he could have at that moment. And definitely safer than spending too much time with Alyson.

Chapter Eleven

Alyson walked through the doors of the now familiar Mad Cow Café. The black-and-white painted walls were even starting to grow on her. So was Vera. It was only seven in the morning and the place was packed.

From a corner booth, Jenna waved to get her attention. That was the reason she was there, to meet with Jenna about the charity concert for the camp. They'd discussed it the previous evening at the bonfire, and decided it would be easier to talk at the Mad Cow, without camp responsibilities to distract them.

Alyson sat down across from Jenna and Vera hurried across the room with the coffeepot. Alyson turned her cup and smiled up at the older woman, who no longer treated her like the stranger that had shown up in town.

Alyson was already a part of the community.

And last night her mother had left a message on her cell phone that she was expected to play in Chicago in three weeks. The same weekend as the fund-raiser.

"That's a long face." Vera poured the coffee and dropped a couple of creamers on the table. Her smile was bright for so early in the morning.

Alyson couldn't imagine wearing that smile before noon.

"Sorry, I'm not great at mornings."

Vera laughed. "Honey, you'd better get used to them if you're going to stay around here. You are going to stay, right?"

"I don't know." Alyson stirred creamer into her coffee and ignored the way Jenna watched her, curious and concerned.

"You have to." Vera, not as subtle as Jenna. "Why, honey, we're all itching to get Jason Bradshaw married off. He isn't getting any younger, and he's a pretty decent catch."

Jenna laughed. "If he can remember your name."

"Oh, he's getting better." Vera pulled the order pad out of her apron pocket. "What can I get you girls for breakfast?"

"Poached eggs and toast." Alyson didn't have to open the menu.

"Omelet, hash browns and bacon." Jenna handed the menu back to Vera. "And milk."

"Eating for two." Vera winked and then she was gone, hurrying off to the kitchen, but refilling several cups of coffee along the way.

"Don't let it get to you." Jenna stirred sugar into her coffee. "This is hard to get used to, having just one cup of coffee in the morning."

"I can't imagine."

"About the matchmakers. Don't worry. They're harmless and they all know that it has to be God's will, not theirs. They love you or they wouldn't be trying to pair you up with Jason."

"I'm not anyone's match." Alyson tried to smile, to let the words sound light.

"Of course you are. You have to trust God, Alyson. I don't think you showed up here by accident."

Alyson looked up. "You really think that God, as busy as He is with this messed-up world, looked down and thought about me, and getting me here?"

"I do think that."

Alyson leaned back and it was okay to smile. "Maybe I'm here because God knew I could help with this fund-raiser."

"Maybe."

It felt right. God had brought her here to help

these people. She liked that thought. And she also thought that she might not have found faith if she hadn't come here. It was new faith, but it was real enough for her to know that God would do this for Camp Hope, for Jenna and Adam.

If she put her time here in that box, then it made it easier to leave, easier to deal with what she thought she might feel for Jason. Because she didn't want to miss him when she left and she knew she would.

"I have an idea about the concert." Alyson steered the conversation back to the reason for meeting and Jenna shot her a knowing smile.

"Okay."

"I could work with the kids on a few songs."

"Sounds great to me."

"And they could display their artwork and photographs they've taken. We could do an art show for guests to look at, even bid on."

"Wow, great ideas." Jenna bit down on her bottom lip and then she leaned forward a little. "What about you, Alyson? Are you going to play?"

"I think the children would be the real attraction. People need to see what Camp Hope is all about."

"If you can't…"

She smiled at the young waitress who came

around the corner with their food. She set their plates down in front of them and then promised to refill their coffee cups.

"Jenna, I really don't think I can."

Jenna switched the plates, giving Alyson her eggs. "It's okay. If you can help the kids and help me get the invitations out to the right people, I think that's going to be more than enough."

"Of course I'll do that." She buttered her toast and started to take a bite, but she put it down on the plate. "I want you to understand. It isn't that I don't want to. I just can't. And I'm not sure if I'll even be able to be here for the fund-raiser."

"I forgot that you mentioned that. It got lost in Vera trying to marry you off to Jason." Jenna put her fork down. "Why would you leave?"

"I have a career. As much as I don't want it, I can't walk away and leave everyone in a lurch."

Jenna nodded, thoughtful and sweet.

"I understand."

"I love it here, though." Alyson looked around the room, at tables full of people she had gotten to know. "I'm so glad I found this place, and found my family."

"Why can't you finish your obligations and come back home, to all of us?"

"I've thought about it."

"And you don't know if you will?"

Alyson shrugged. "I'm not sure. I came here looking for my family and I've found them. I know that I'll never lose them. But I have an apartment and I have my family in Boston."

There was so much she hadn't planned on. She hadn't planned on having a twin. She hadn't planned on Camp Hope. She definitely hadn't planned on Jason.

There were no easy answers for her future.

The arena was empty. Jason walked through the double doors, glad for a few minutes alone. He had seen the kids going from the dining hall to their dorms. He had a few minutes to get his act together and to get ready for the kids who were going to try their hands at steer riding.

He needed to be thinking about them, not about Alyson standing next to the bonfire last night, the glow of the flames flickering in her eyes. And when he'd dropped her off at home, she'd thanked him and walked inside. He remembered standing there in the cool evening air, with nothing.

He flipped on the lights and the arena changed from a dusky place, shadowy and quiet, to bright and ready for action. From a pen at the other end of the building low mooing erupted.

He walked along the outside edge of the arena to the pens where steers were being held. He flaked off hay and tossed it in. The steers, rangy and young, ran to the back of the pen. They eyed him, snorting and wide-eyed, and then came forward again, taking bites of hay.

They had water. Now they had food. And he had time on his hands.

He turned away from the steers as Adam and Clint led a group of about twenty kids into the arena. Adam pointed to the small riser of bleacher-type seats and the kids filed single file down the row and took seats.

"This is what we're going to do today." Adam leaned against the gate and addressed the kids. "Our rodeo is in a little over a week. You've learned to ride. You've learned to rope. And today we're going to put a few of you on steers. But before we do, Jason is going to do a demonstration on a bull."

Adam shot him a look. "You up to that?"

Jason shrugged. "Ready as I'll ever be."

Clint ran a bull into one of the chutes and held Jason's bull rope up for the teens to see it. "Here you go."

Jason walked to the chute, rethinking his involvement in this, in teaching kids, in the camp, and bull riding. He had a nice piece of land, some livestock, a great house. Why in the world was he still riding bulls?

His dad had always said that someone needed to pound some sense into him. A couple of months ago, a bull had tried. So where was that sense? Shouldn't he be handing the rope to Clint, telling him to go for it, or find someone a little younger to climb on that big, red bull snorting in the chute.

The bull was one of Willow's older bulls. The animal snorted and pawed. It rammed against the metal gate and bellowed. Clint laughed a little as Jason stood on the platform overlooking the animal. Nearly a ton of bone-breaking ability caged inside a metal chute and about to be unleashed on him.

He hadn't been on a bull since the accident. He'd been on the mechanical bull at the camp. The kids had trained with him on it. He'd taught them the basics and knew their skill level would match the steers they were going up against today.

The steers were a third the size of and not nearly the man this bull was.

"If you're not ready?" Clint had his bull rope ready and Jason had to make the move.

"I'm ready." Jason climbed over the gate,

trying not to think about the ride that had changed his life and how it had felt before he climbed on the back of that bull. He didn't remember the ride, just the way the animal snorted as he lowered onto its back.

He remembered the music. He lowered himself onto the back of the bull with Clint leaning over him, ready to pull the rope and help him get it tight.

Heavy metal music had been playing the night he got trampled into a hard-packed dirt arena in Arizona. There was no music today. The bull shifted beneath him, lowering its massive head and then leaning into the gate, pushing Jason's leg into the metal. Adam Mackenzie pushed from the outside of the gate, the arena side, moving the bull.

The rope was tight. Clint handed him the end and Jason wrapped it around his hand. The moment of truth. Could he get back into an arena without losing his nerve? When the gate opened, would he jump before the bull made its first jump?

Jason felt the bull settle. He nodded and Adam opened the gate. The bull turned out, bursting into the arena with two thousand pounds of fury and force. It bucked, hopped to the side and rolled its back a little to the left before settling into a spin that included a front jump with each revolution.

A few jumps felt as if the animal's back end was trying to meet up with its front end. Jason gritted his teeth and clenched his hand a little tighter. His spine felt like it was being jammed into his brain.

Jason didn't wait for the eight-second buzzer. He loosened his hand from the rope and waited for the right moment to jump, knowing Clint and Adam would distract the bull as he fell to the ground.

When he landed, he landed on his feet, lost his balance and fell to his knees, but the bull was there, head just inches away, snorting, blowing hot air at Jason. He got to his feet, helped by Adam grabbing the back of his Kevlar vest. Clint pushed the head of the raging animal, giving Jason a few seconds to recover and climb the gate, out of the arena.

Alyson didn't realize how tightly her hands were clenched in her lap until Jenna patted her on the back and whispered for her to relax. As if she could. Her heart was pounding so hard she didn't know if it would ever return to its normal beat and she'd bitten into her bottom lip hard enough that it was probably bleeding.

That man who had sat on the back of that bull was a Jason Bradshaw she'd never met. He wasn't the same cowboy with the quick smile and easy laugh that she knew. This man was dead serious about his sport and willing to go head to head with a two-thousand-pound animal.

As he limped out of the arena, she moved toward him, but Jenna grabbed her arm. "Not yet. Let him throw something or kick something."

"But what if he's hurt?" Alyson watched him walk out the gate, past the chutes and out a side door.

"He isn't hurt. He's mad because he didn't make the eight seconds. He's mad at his body for letting him down."

Alyson tried to get it, but it was a world far removed from the one she'd always lived in.

Clint was standing in the arena, talking to the kids who had showed up for their first day of riding real steers. The kids—all teenagers— were leaning forward, catching every word, bouncing with excitement.

"I'll be back." Alyson stood up and Jenna let her go. She walked down metal steps that vibrated with each movement.

With every step she questioned why she was doing this. He had friends. These people understood him. They knew when he needed to be left alone.

But maybe he'd convinced them that alone was where he belonged.

What did she know about the life of a bull rider? Or the life of a cowboy? She looked down, at the boots that were starting to look a little worn. She was breaking in her country self, feeling more like Alyson Forester.

Jason was in the stable, pulling a saddle out of the tack room. He turned when she walked up. His smile spread easily across his face, but it didn't reach his eyes, didn't leave the crinkles at the corners that she was so used to.

"That was pretty amazing." She leaned against the wall, relieved that he couldn't see the way her insides shook.

"Yeah, amazing. At least I remember your name." He winked and picked up the saddle. She followed him to a stall that held a pretty black horse.

"That's good to know." She reached to pet the nose of the horse. "Are you okay?"

He turned, still smiling. "Of course I am."

"Okay." But she knew he wasn't. Of course he wasn't. He smiled. He made jokes. He deflected. "Are you going for a ride, now? I mean, aren't you going to stay and teach the kids to ride the steers?"

He put the saddle down. "I don't know."

"Oh."

"I can't even believe I'm here, teaching kids at a camp."

"Did it ever occur to you that we're supposed to be here?" She took a step closer, liking that he smelled like soap and peppermint. "I'm here because my life fell apart. You're here because your career got put on hold. But we both needed to be here."

He shook his head and then smiled, reaching out, but he didn't take her hand. And she had wanted him to. Instead, he shoved his hand into his pocket.

"Thank you." He leaned, his hands still in his pocket, and he dropped a kiss on her cheek. "You're right."

"But that doesn't make it any easier."

He laughed. "Not really, but it was sweet. Let's go teach some boys to ride bulls."

He hooked his finger through her belt loop and his first step tugged her back. She glanced to the side, catching the grimace of pain.

"Do you think you need to go…?"

He shook his head. "Not yet. Let's get this camp over, and then I'll get it taken care of."

"Right."

They walked back into the arena and Alyson walked up the steps to where Jenna was still sitting. Jason joined the guys. They had a steer in a chute and an older teen, not from the camp, standing on the platform, about to climb on the back of the animal. The steer, red-coated and thrashing his head back and forth, started bucking inside the chute, before the boy could get settled on his back.

Jason hauled the kid out by the back of his shirt.

"I'm not sure if I can watch." Alyson covered her face, but she peeked through her fingers.

Jenna's laughter was soft. "You get used to it. You have to understand that these guys know what they're doing. And the guys in the arena, they're tops at keeping a rider safe. They'll jump between the bull and the bull rider. That's the job of a bull fighter."

"They don't really fight the bull?"

"No, they distract him. They're in there to keep that cowboy safe. They'll pull him loose if his hand gets hung up in the rope. They'll jerk him off the ground and give him a shove if he needs it. I've seen them cover a fallen bull rider with their own bodies to keep the guy safe from those hooves."

"That's pretty amazing. And the kids from the camp are wearing helmets?"

Jenna nodded. "Helmets and Kevlar vests. Bull riders started wearing the bulletproof vest after Lane Frost got killed. A lot of cowboys have been saved by that vest."

Alyson let out a breath and told herself to relax. But her gaze kept going to Jason Bradshaw. She kept thinking of him on the back of that bull.

And she realized she would have jumped in there and saved him.

It felt as if he had already rescued her.

Jenna and Alyson left before Jason finished up with the kids. He had walked out of the arena and they were gone. From the distance he heard the piano in the chapel and he thought she might be there.

Rather than going there, to her, he left for the day. He hadn't been home before dark all week. And tonight he was moving back into his house. He could finish a sentence. He could remember where he was going, most of the time.

And he needed his house, his space.

He parked outside the garage and eased himself out of the truck. Hopping out was no longer the recommended exit strategy. He leaned against the truck for a minute and then turned and walked out to the barn. Someone was already there.

When Beth walked out, she smiled. He breathed out a sigh, because it was easy to see her now. The bruises were long gone. Her arm had healed. He didn't know about her heart. But she was smiling, and that counted for something.

"What are you doing here?" He stopped at the gate.

"I didn't know you'd be here so early. I was feeding for you. You have a new foal."

"The bay mare?"

Beth nodded in the direction of the twenty-acre field south of his barn. "Yeah, and she looks like her mother."

"That's what I hoped for. Let's walk out and take a look."

"I can't. I promised Dad we'd run into Tulsa tonight. It's a little funny, but I think he feels bad for Marcie Ballentine."

"Dad and Marcie with the five kids?"

"That's the one." Beth pushed dark-brown hair back from her face, revealing the one scar that hadn't disappeared with time, right above her eye. "The kids are all grown. It isn't like he'd be raising them."

"Yeah, I guess. What does this have to do with Tulsa?"

"She's going with us. He says it's the neighborly thing to do, to take out a neighbor who is down."

"Wow." Jason latched the gate they had walked through. The grass was a little long. He'd had fewer horses on it than normal and it hadn't been eaten down the way it usually would have been by this time of the year.

The mare grazed and her foal, still damp and wobbly, stood at her side, trying to find dinner. Jason stopped, not wanting to interrupt.

"Pretty, isn't she?"

"She is." He smiled, because his thoughts took a sudden turn and he wasn't seeing the foal, it was Alyson's face that flashed through his mind, taking him by surprise.

Then again, it didn't surprise him.

Chapter Twelve

Alyson stuck a needle through the back of the cloth and pulled the thread through, adding another touch of color to what she hoped would be her first finished needlepoint. She'd been working on it all week, each night after she got home from camp.

Her grandmother had told her it was a relaxing pastime. That had sounded good after watching Jason ride the bull at camp.

Alyson poked the needle through again and this time it got hung up, the way it had been doing all evening, tangling thread at the back of what was supposed to be a picture of a cottage.

"You're supposed to relax when you're doing this." Etta laughed, but she didn't stop the movement of the spinning wheel. She'd bought wool and she was busy turning it into yarn. That was something else Alyson couldn't do. She couldn't spin. She'd tried and the ensuing tangle of wool had made her grandmother grumble just a little.

"I'm relaxed." She jabbed the needle through the cloth again. "Ouch."

She kissed her finger and put the needlepoint down on the table next to her. She loved this attic room with the tall eaves, the stained-glass window and the window seat. It was a fairy tale room. She hoped she wouldn't prick her finger and sleep for one hundred years.

Because there weren't any handsome princes out searching for her—she was sure of that.

Not even a cowboy. Because the cowboy had gone off to a rodeo, just days before camp ended. A rodeo in Oklahoma City, where he hoped to garner points that would help him get back on track for the world championship.

"What's your mother up to? Didn't she call earlier?" Etta kept spinning, but cast a look back, over her shoulder.

"She called."

"She's been calling a lot."

"I know. She's reminding me that I have a career and I can't be gone forever." Alyson picked up the needlepoint again, but she didn't pick up the needle. "She reminded me that I have a concert in Chicago. In fifteen days."

The same weekend as the fund-raiser for Camp Hope. No amount of needlepoint was going to make her feel better about that, or about leaving.

She was torn between her two lives, and knowing which world she belonged in. She didn't know how to explain to Etta that Gary Anderson had raised her, and that he had been a fair man, buffering her from her mother's tangents.

She couldn't explain to her mother about the faith she had found in Dawson.

"No matter what, Alyson, you have family here. I know you have commitments you have to keep. That can't be undone, but she can't take Dawson out of you. You can take the girl out of the country, but you sure can't take the country out of the girl." Etta stopped spinning. "And you can't take her faith, either."

"I know." Alyson jabbed at the fabric again, fighting tears that clouded her vision. "It shouldn't be this difficult."

She closed her eyes, trying to breathe past the tightness in her throat and then she blinked away the tears.

Where would she put her new life, this new

person she'd become, when she went back to Boston? Her heart ached, thinking about how it would feel to lose the person she'd become.

She wouldn't lose herself. She pulled the needle through the fabric again, adding another block to the chimney of the cottage. She was Alyson Forester. Alyson Anderson had ceased to be. That Alyson had been the creation of her mother.

The new Alyson knew what she wanted from her life. She knew who she was. That wouldn't change.

"Let's go downstairs and bake something." Etta's other antidote for stress. "Pizza."

Alyson laughed. "I think not."

A car rumbled up the drive. Etta got up to go look, "Maybe Andie is home early."

"That would be good."

"Nope, it's Jason Bradshaw. Imagine that."

Alyson didn't have to imagine. Not much. She'd been thinking about him all day. She glanced out the window and watched him get out of the truck that pulled a horse trailer.

"What's he doing?" Etta turned from the window. "I've never known that boy to be so hard to figure out. He's always been a pretty carefree guy."

Alyson couldn't agree with that comment.

She thought that he'd always pretended to be carefree and that maybe no one had ever figured him out the way she had. Maybe they'd all been so glad to see him smiling, joking, being the great guy they all relied on, that no one had given him the chance to be the man she thought he might be.

Days ago he had whispered that he wanted her to know him. And she thought she did.

Jason led the Appaloosa gelding out of the trailer and tied him to the side. He went back in after his horse. When he turned from tying the big roan to the trailer, Alyson was standing behind him. He grinned and pushed his hat back.

"Thought you might like to go for a ride."

She looked up, at the dusky evening sky. "It's late."

"Only eight o'clock. It's the only time of day that's really cool enough for a longer ride."

He looked down at her flip-flops and back up, catching her smile. Her toenails were cotton candy pink and she wore a toe ring.

"I'd have to change."

"So change." He rested his arm on the rump of his red roan. The horse moved to the side a little and stomped at a fly. "I'll get these guys saddled and ready to go, you grab us a couple of bottles of water."

"And change."

He grinned. "Sure, but I really like the pink polish."

She turned about the same color as her nails and then she recovered. "You can borrow it."

He laughed and the horse moved abruptly to the right, knocking him off balance. "I think I'll leave the polish for you. We can share that way. You wear it, and I'll enjoy it."

"I'll be back."

He watched as she hurried up the sidewalk and then he turned back to the roan.

"Buddy, this isn't something a guy plans." The horse looked back and reached to nip at his arm. Jason pushed the horse away. "I don't think so."

He was saddling the Appaloosa when Alyson walked out the front door with Etta. He glanced back over his shoulder, catching a glimpse of Alyson and then returning his attention to the horse, tightening the girth strap, fiddling with the stirrups, whatever it took.

"I'm making brownies." Etta stopped next to the roan. "They'll be ready when you get back."

"Sounds great." His gaze traveled to Alyson. She had changed into a T-shirt and jeans. The toenails were no longer in sight. He was a little sorry about that. Maybe they should have put off riding and just sat on the porch with coffee and brownies.

"Ready?" Her tone was hesitant and she moved a little toward the Appaloosa, a dark almost black horse with a white blanket on its rump. The horse turned, nuzzling at her, a good fit for a beginning rider. He'd borrowed the gelding from Adam and Jenna.

"I'm ready. Do you have the…"

She held up two bottles of water. "Water?"

"Yep." He untied her horse and led it away from the trailer.

Alyson took the reins and grabbed the saddle horn. He cupped his hands for her foot and she ignored him. She slid her left foot into the stirrup and swung her right leg over the saddle.

"I can do it, but thanks." She grinned down at him.

He saluted and went to his horse. Etta was at the porch. She turned and watched, waving. And she looked worried. Jason felt that look in the pit of his stomach as he pulled himself onto his horse, settling in the saddle and glancing back at Alyson to make sure she was okay.

She looked as worried as Etta.

"Where to?" She eased her horse up next to his as they took off down the road.

"Church."

"Okay, that's strange."

He smiled a little. "They're having a trail ride from there."

"Oh, so it isn't just the two of us?" She looked away before he could see if the look on her face was disappointment or relief.

"No, not just the two of us. Maybe a dozen." All couples. He didn't tell her that part. That he'd made them a couple for this ride.

This was courting, Dawson-style.

The Appaloosa gelding was an easy horse to ride. He poked along, not too doggy, but Alyson didn't have to constantly control him, or worry about him. His head was up, ears pricked attentively.

"Nice horse." She eased into the ride, losing her nervousness, until she saw the crowd at the church. Not a crowd really, but a group, and all couples.

"It's a couples' ride." Jason shot her a grin that remained in his eyes, crinkling at the corners. And she didn't know what to say.

"Alyson, it isn't a big deal. It's just an easy way for people to get together, to do something on a muggy summer night when the Mad Cow—fine dining that it is—is closed. No one really wants to drive to Grove, or to Tulsa. We'll ride down the road, maybe stop at the creek to water the horses, and ride back."

"It does sound like fun."

Because Jason wasn't afraid of her. He didn't stumble, trying to find the right words. He wanted to spend time with her.

The others greeted them. One of the riders was Etta's neighbor. She couldn't remember his name, but he was rowdy and full of himself. She'd seen him talking to Andie and then he'd hopped in the truck with some pretty brunette and taken off.

Andie said he was her best friend. Alyson thought her sister might be fooling herself. And she was surprised to see him at church. She hadn't seen him there before.

"If everyone's ready, we can go." The guy on a big white horse rode to the front of the group.

Alyson turned her horse, looking for Jason. He rode up next to her, his smile easy, chasing away the nervousness that fluttered in her stomach.

"How was your rodeo?" she asked as they headed down the dirt road behind the church. She'd never seen a dirt road until she came here.

It was magical, riding down that tree-lined road, and dusk falling over the Oklahoma countryside. Horses plodded along, their hooves beating a rhythmic tune on the road, tails swishing.

"I didn't win." He shrugged as if it didn't matter. "I think I'm done. It hit me while I was out there. I've always been on the road. I didn't know what else to do with my life. And now I've found something else."

She glanced up, meeting brown eyes that were melted chocolate on a summer night.

"The camp." He smiled. "And a new friend. Leaving home isn't as much fun as it used to be."

When he was running. When it had been too much to be at home, with his dad hurting and his sister in California with an abusive husband. It had been hard to be at home then. She didn't say it, because it was his story and he knew.

But her grandmother had been wrong about one thing. Finding out his story wasn't fun. It was difficult, and it hurt to learn what his smile had hidden.

But she had also learned that Jason smiled because he had faith. He didn't let things keep him down, she realized. That's what his smile was all about. It was about dealing with whatever was going on in his life and finding the answers.

She wanted it to be that easy for her. But she felt torn, pulled in two directions. She loved her family, both sides of it. God had been working on her, healing her heart, helping her to remember good things about her parents, not just the deception and the pressure.

"It can't be easy to walk away from." She meant his bull riding, but it sounded like she meant her own life as well. They had similar stories. "It's been a big part of your life."

He rode close and their knees brushed. His horse bit at hers and he pulled the gelding away. "I've had a couple of months to adjust. I've learned that it's okay to give it up."

"That's good."

They rode through an open gate and into a field. A deer jumped out of a stand of trees and raced across the field. Alyson pulled back on the reins and watched. A fawn followed the mother, jumping and darting across the field.

"I have to leave." There, she'd said it. The words were loud in the silence of that summer evening.

"Leave what?"

"I have concerts that I have to play or it'll leave everyone in a bind." Obligations that she'd run from, but she had to stop running.

She'd found herself. Now she had to literally go face the music.

"I see." He pulled his horse up and she

stopped next to him. "What about the concert for Camp Hope?"

"I have a concert that weekend in Chicago. I'm going to try and make it back. I just don't know if I can."

The perfect summer evening crumbled in around her. Jason pushed his hat back and then he shrugged, like it didn't matter. And he didn't say that he would miss her. He didn't ask her to stay.

It felt as if he had always planned on her leaving.

It shouldn't have bothered him so much. Jason was still telling himself that as they rode back to the church an hour later. A perfect summer evening, riding with a woman he'd come to know in a way he hadn't expected, and now this.

The great escape artist had had the tables turned on him.

She was the one leaving.

"Jason, I don't want to lose you."

He pulled his horse up next to the trailer and dismounted. She landed on the ground next to her horse, standing there in her Dawson persona, he thought. She had easily turned herself from Boston to Dawson in a matter of weeks.

And turned his life pretty much upside down in the process. His memory problems had been nothing compared to this. As a matter of fact, he almost wished for memory loss, so he could walk away and close the door on this relationship.

She tied her horse to the side of the trailer and stepped around his horse, putting herself next to him. "I came here looking for my family, and for myself. You were a big part of that journey."

"Right." He led his horse to the back of the trailer and turned to look at her. He felt about sixteen and she was the prom queen. But she'd never been to a prom. To a dance.

She'd been everywhere, but nowhere.

"Alyson, I…" He wasn't about to say it. The words settled in his stomach and crawled around like yesterday's lunch. He would bite his tongue before he told her he thought he might love her. He wasn't going to keep her here that way, with words. It had to be more than words.

He couldn't say it, not without really knowing. But he thought he knew. And the idea of her leaving made it all the more clear.

But he wouldn't do that to her, either. He wouldn't make her feel guilty for doing what she had to do.

"You what?" She leaned against the trailer, watching him. Her booted foot was on the rail and her hair had come loose from the clip on top of her head.

"Nothing." He leaned in and kissed her cheek. It wasn't enough, that sweet kiss, but he wasn't going any further in this relationship. "We should get home."

Chapter Thirteen

Alyson met with Jenna two mornings after that ride with Jason. They sat under the shade tree, watching kids play a game of baseball. Timmy and David were in the middle of it all, keeping the older kids laughing.

"So, you're leaving?"

Alyson nodded. She sighed, because the decision was a heavy weight on her heart. Jenna had become such a good friend, probably the best friend Alyson had ever had. But she was another friend that Alyson would have to walk away from. Because her family needed her.

Her entire life had been about what her family needed. Their lifestyle depended on her, had depended on her since they learned about her gift.

She didn't want to resent her talent. This gift that God had given her. She could see that now. So what did she do with it? How did she go forward, with a new faith, and a new attitude?

How did she go back to Boston with this faith?

She leaned forward, petting Jenna's dog named Dog. Or Puppy. Or Buddy. It depended on who you asked.

"Yes, I have to go." She scrunched her fingers through the silky soft fur at the dog's neck and wrinkled her nose because the animal had been into something and he smelled like a garbage dump. She pulled back and he nudged her with his nose.

"Go away, dog." Jenna pushed him back. "I think he got into the kitchen trash again. You'll come back, though. Right?"

Back to their conversation. "I don't know when, but I want to come back. I plan on it."

"Getting married, having a few kids?"

Alyson laughed. "Buying an old house, being the crazy cat lady."

"Right, staying single, not falling in love." Jenna shook her head. "Keep telling yourself that."

She would have to keep telling herself that, because she didn't know her future. She didn't know when or how she would come back to

Dawson. First she had to deal with the past and with the career that had been hers for as long as she could remember.

And now her father was trying to get her a record deal. She remembered a time when that had been her dream. Or at least it had been the dream her mother had put in her mind.

"It makes it easier to leave." Alyson stood up. "I have a few kids meeting me in the chapel for their last piano lesson."

"Thank you for doing that with them." Jenna stood up, groaning in the process. "This kid can't come soon enough."

"I wouldn't have missed working here for anything. And Jenna, if I can, I'll get back in time for the charity concert. And if you need anything, just call. I'll do what I can from the road."

"Thanks. I know this isn't easy for you. And believe me, I'll call."

"Good, because I'm going to miss you."

"We'll all miss you, Alyson. All of us."

Everyone would miss her.

Alyson walked away, down the path to the chapel. She saw the few kids with their camp counselor heading toward the chapel. They waved and she waved back.

Could this be the new plan, the new way of using her talent? The idea lightened her mood.

She loved these children. She loved teaching them and watching them. What would it be like, to trade a career, a record deal, for this life?

What would they all say if she went home and told them she was through?

If it wasn't for obligations, she would have done just that. She wouldn't even have gone home; she would have called.

She would stay and be the crazy cat lady who taught local children to play piano. She smiled as she walked through the doors of the chapel. She loved that scenario. She could picture herself in a little house with a veranda, wicker furniture, and Etta stopping by to visit. She could see herself in her grandmother's tie-dyed clothing, wearing big floppy hats and weeding her flower garden.

If only. It seemed as if her life had become a pattern of If Only.

The other thing she thought about was being onstage again. Sitting on the stage under bright lights, knowing the crowd sat in darkness, listening. Fear tightened in her chest and she breathed to release it.

She wasn't going to fear. She no longer had to fear. If she kept telling herself, she might believe it. She might believe that she wasn't afraid to leave here.

She couldn't be afraid to face the world. Not now. She had prayed about it, and as new as prayer was to her, she had to believe that God wasn't going to stay in this town, letting her face the world alone. He would be with her. No matter where she went.

The kids pulled her forward, out of her thoughts, and into their presence, where there was no room for fear. She let them lead her down the aisle to the piano. Their counselor, a woman from their home church, tried to calm them down.

"It's okay." Alyson hugged them close. "As soon as we start playing, they'll calm down."

They always did.

And so did she, now that she was playing for herself.

"Who's going first today?" Alyson asked.

Becky, a girl of about twelve, raised her hand. "Can I? I've been practicing."

"Go ahead." Alyson sat on the bench with the girl. They were working on simple songs. Of course they wouldn't learn a lot in two weeks of camp. But Alyson's hope was that they would go home and find a way to continue. She had talked to the youth pastor of the church about helping to find teachers in their area who might donate their time to needy children.

The girl played through the page of the book they'd been working on. As she played, Alyson looked up, catching sight of someone at the entrance to the chapel.

Jason. He tipped his hat and nodded. And then he walked away.

Jason walked out to the arena. In fifteen minutes Jenna would join him and they'd work with a group of girls who were going to barrel race in the rodeo, and the winner would come back in two weeks for the charity event.

He had fifteen minutes to get a lot of crazy out of his system. He really didn't like crazy. He'd had years of practicing keeping his cool, keeping his emotions under wraps.

To lose it now really didn't sit well with him.

Because of a woman. Man, how in the world had that happened?

As he walked through the stable, he found Adam. "Could you work the controls for me?"

"The bull?"

"What else."

"I thought you were giving that up." Adam closed the door to the tack room.

"I am. Or was. Who knows?"

"Hey, it's your choice." Adam led the way into the arena. The overhead lights were off. It was hot and a little dusty. Barrels had been set out in a triangle pattern for the girls who would be practicing.

Adam left his side and walked back to the control panel for the bull.

Jason grabbed a glove and walked over to the mechanical bull. He climbed on, cringing a little with the effort of actually swinging his knee. He settled onto the back of the bull and wrapped his hand in the rope.

It wasn't a real bull. It didn't stomp. It didn't rear up in the chute and try to cram his head into the gate. It wasn't going to try to lie down or roll over in a narrow enclosure with him on its back.

It was safe. When had he become about safe? He pounded his hand into the rope and pushed his hat down tight on his head.

All his frustration settled deep inside him. He would work it out on the back of a machine that couldn't really fight back. But he could fight through. This was familiar. He knew how to control this. He knew how to keep it together on the back of a bull.

And control felt good, even if it was this one thing, this moment.

He nodded his head and Adam gave the bull a crank and a twist. Jason felt the jolt, got strung out, his arm in the rope straightening and his left arm, his free arm going backward, jerking his body back, forcing him to lose his seat.

His head snapped forward and he fought to get control of his upper body. Chin tucked, he broke at the hips, bringing himself back to center on the next jump. The bull spun and he anticipated the move, holding steady, bringing himself forward when momentum tried to take him back again.

The bull slowed to a stop. He didn't have to jump, didn't have to escape pounding hooves or horns that would hit a guy upside the head. Instead, he climbed off. And for the first time since April, his vision refocused without dizziness, without spinning. His head didn't pound.

He limped off the platform and across the arena, remembering how it felt to be in an arena with a crowd, with a real bull blowing hot air down his neck and kicking dirt into his face as he rolled away from pounding hooves. He pushed his hat, loosening it, and looked up, meeting Adam's curious gaze.

"Well?" Adam asked.

"I'm only seeing one of you and I still remember where I am."

"I mean, did that solve your problems?"

"Nope." Because he could ride a bull but he couldn't shake a woman from his mind. He was no longer a love 'em and leave 'em kind of guy. It was a bad time to figure that out, when the woman in question was making plans to leave.

But maybe it wasn't her. Maybe it was just settling down that mattered.

He could date and find someone who wanted to settle down with him in Dawson, on a ranch, with a few horses, some cattle and a couple of kids.

Somehow that version of the future didn't make him feel better, either.

"The kids are on their way down." Jason could see them heading toward the stable, a handful of girls and Jenna.

He had considered bull riding again. But being here, at this camp. That was okay, too. Having his ranch, and really living there, also a pretty good feeling.

Nope, going on the road wasn't in his plans at all.

And before long, Alyson Forester would be a memory. He had kind of hoped he would forget her, but he'd never been able to forget Alyson.

Alyson left on Monday after the last day of camp and the rodeo. She had wanted to watch the final performance of kids whose lives she had been involved with. And it had been the best night of her life, watching those kids perform with confidence.

And now it was time to go. She stood on the porch with Etta, hugging her grandmother tight. A yellow house, lavender wicker furniture, and a woman who loved her, no matter what. Unconditional love, something she'd learned in Dawson. Alyson held on to her grandmother, and the moment.

She tried not to think about Jason.

"You don't have to go." Etta walked down the stairs with her, across the lawn to the car.

Alyson's kitten ran across the lawn, brushing against her legs, tail twitching. She picked it up and held it close. She couldn't look at her grandmother. If Etta had tears in her eyes, Alyson knew she would cry, too.

She thought she'd probably cry anyway.

But she had to go. She had to face her fears. That's what it had come down to.

"I have to go." Alyson put the kitten down and opened the trunk of her car. She had packed up last night, but she had her overnight bag to store. There were more clothes than she'd come with. Her new wardrobe, clothes that made her a part of Dawson, less a part of Boston.

She closed the trunk and turned to face her

grandmother, facing her tears. "I have to go. I have to face my fears. I have to face my parents and forgive them. I have to talk to my sister Laura. I want her to know that it's okay. She loves Dan. He loves her. They should be together."

"Will it be that easy?" Etta put an arm around Alyson's waist and pulled her close, hugging her again.

"It won't be that easy, but I've forgiven her. And I do love my mom. I know she loved us the best way she knew how."

She refused to acknowledge the smiling face that flashed through her mind. She refused to let herself think about him, about not talking to him for days, other than casual greetings as they passed one another at the camp. And she reminded herself of Andie's warnings, that he'd break her heart.

But it wasn't his fault. She'd made a decision to leave. But she would come back to Dawson. Maybe someday she'd come back and be the crazy cat lady who taught children to play the piano.

But first she had to be Alyson Anderson, pianist. Even if being that person scared her to death, shook her insides and made her want to run away, again.

"You're stronger than you realize, Aly." Etta kissed her cheek. "You're an amazing young woman and I'm proud of you. I'm proud that you're not running from your commitments. I'm proud of you for facing your fears. But don't forget that you have family in Dawson."

"I won't forget." She couldn't forget. Memories were strong and she knew that each time she smelled honeysuckle or petunias, she'd think of home. She'd think of Etta.

And each time she saw a man with an easy smile, she'd feel her heart break all over again.

"Goodbye, sweetie." Etta backed away from the car.

"I love you." Alyson got into the car and Etta closed the door.

Jason watched Alyson drive out of town, but he didn't go after her. Alyson had fears to conquer and she had a life that didn't include any of them. He had to let her go.

Even if it wasn't easy.

He walked into the Mad Cow and sat down at a table with a half-dozen local ranchers. They stopped talking when he sat down. But Clint Cameron finally spoke up.

"So, you're just going to let her leave?"

"She's a big girl." Jason turned his coffee cup

over for the waitress to fill it. She pulled out her order pad and he shook his head. "Just coffee."

"Right." Johnny Foster laughed. "And you're an idiot if you let her leave."

"She's already gone." Wasn't that a country song? He shook it off and slid his attention back to the cup of coffee. He sipped the hot, black liquid.

"She doesn't have to be," Clint interjected.

"You know, I'd really like to talk about something other than Alyson." Jason pushed his coffee cup back. "I have to leave."

"Jason, come on. We're cool." Johnny Foster laughed. "It's just that we don't always have the chance to give you a hard time—not over a woman. We've never seen you like this."

"Right." Jason walked out the door, without a joke, without a comment to make things okay for his friends.

He didn't have a thing to say that would make anyone laugh. He was done trying to hide behind a smile. People expected him to always be okay, to roll with whatever hit him.

And he didn't think he could roll with this. The thought knocked him on his can.

Clint walked out the door, catching up with him. "You know, you could go after her."

"No, I can't."

"Send her roses. Make sure she knows that you're here when she decides it's time to come back."

"Is that what you did?" Jason pulled his keys out of his pocket, half wanting the answer, half wanting to sound like it didn't really matter, as if he didn't really mean it.

"No, I gave Willow room to be strong. I helped her realize she could make it. Oh, and that she couldn't stand to live without me."

"Right, well, Alyson is going back to Boston. She's going to return to the stage and be who she was meant to be. And that's her choice. That's me letting her be strong."

"And you think you're going to just stop loving her?"

A conversation between two cowboys shouldn't take this direction, that's what Jason thought. It sounded like an episode of *Oprah* or like some sappy chick flick that made women cry.

"You know, Clint, I realize you're married and Willow has helped you get in touch with your emotions, but I'm still kind of not so much into the whole touchy-feely stuff. So if you don't mind, I'm going to head to the ranch and ride a bull."

Because that felt like a man's way to deal with emotions when things got a little touchy-feely.

Clint laughed. And even though Jason laughed as he got into his truck, his mind kept running back to the word *love*.

Chapter Fourteen

Alyson walked next to her mother through the concert hall in Chicago. It hadn't been an easy reunion. Alyson really thought that her mother would never understand the pain she'd caused. Her mother would never get that being a concert pianist had never been Alyson's dream.

But something good had come from all this. Alyson could now look at her family through eyes that saw more clearly. They didn't need her. Her father had a business managing musicians from all over the country.

For years Alyson's mother had told her that they depended on her. Maybe they had. They had needed her to build this business. They had needed her in the spotlight.

Now they didn't.

"What about your grandmother? Is she going to be here?" Caroline Anderson had held on to bitterness. It laced her tone, settled in her eyes.

"She has the flu. Andie is at home with her."

Andie, your other daughter, Alyson wanted to remind her mother. She let it go, because she knew their mother couldn't be pushed.

They'd had the conversation. Alyson had tried to get her mother to talk about Andie, about leaving her and taking Alyson. But the conversations had ended with Caroline saying she had done the best she could and hadn't Andie had a good life.

"I'm sorry she's sick. Alyson, about this recording contract. This is a chance that few people ever get. It's a once-in-a-lifetime opportunity."

"I don't want it. I didn't have a choice when I was younger, but now I do. This isn't my life."

"This is about Etta and Dawson. You're not thinking clearly." Her mother looked away. "I should have thrown that paperwork away. You wouldn't have known about them if I hadn't kept it. But I thought someday..."

"You knew that someday I'd want to know the truth."

"Yes." Her mom turned back around, her

eyes swimming with unshed tears. "Whatever else you believe, you have to know I love you."

"I love you, too. But Mom, I love Dawson. I love a cowboy from Dawson. That's going to be my life."

"I understand, Alyson. I loved a cowboy from Dawson, too."

The words were whispered between them, it wasn't perfect, but it was a start.

"There's your sister." Caroline stepped away, straightening her jacket and it seemed as if she straightened her emotions, pulling herself together emotionally with that movement.

Laura walked down the hall to greet them, looking shy, young. And Alyson didn't resent her. Her sister was beautiful, with curly blond hair and a face that was beautiful and sweet. She'd never been a bad person, never mean. She'd always laughed and teased.

The wedding ring on her finger glinted in the lights of the hallway, mocking Alyson. But she wouldn't let it be about what had happened, not when they had saved her from a huge mistake.

"Alyson."

"Laura." Alyson took the first stop, hugging her sister. "I'm glad you're here."

Laura started to cry. "I'm so sorry. I should

have talked to you. I should have told you how I felt. How Dan felt."

"You should have. It should have been more than a note, Laura. That hurt."

"I know that now. I hope you'll forgive me. Forgive us."

"I've already forgiven you." Because Alyson had experienced forgiveness. She knew how it felt, that moment when she learned that God had forgiven her. She knew how mercy felt.

She closed her eyes. And she knew how love felt. Her heart had been tripping all over that reality for a week. She had tried to tell herself that love didn't happen in weeks. In that short amount of time, she couldn't know a person so well that she thought he might be someone she wanted to spend her life with. But she did know Jason. And she knew without question that she loved him.

Did it really matter? He had let her go. He hadn't tried to stop her, or called to see if she would come back. She didn't know what that meant, but she knew what she felt. And when he had held her, it had felt like he might love her back.

If she went back to Dawson, what if he wasn't there? What if he had decided to go back on the road?

She could question herself all night and make herself doubt what she really wanted. She had made up her mind. No matter what, she was going back to Dawson. Even if she was just going back to work at Camp Hope, she was going back.

Tonight, though, she was going to face her fears. She was going to conquer this stage. She was going to be strong. This wasn't like before, when fear had controlled her because she had never felt as if she could be good enough. Now it wasn't about being good enough. It was about doing what she was meant to do.

She stood offstage and looked at the piano where she'd be performing. The stage was dark and the lights were still on in the auditorium as people took their seats. The symphony was performing tonight and she was their guest. Her mind raced back to the past, to standing in so many spots like this one, waiting.

Fearing.

Even now her heart raced. She remembered how much she'd disliked performing. The music had stopped mattering. It had stopped being an escape. It had become something she wanted to escape from.

And she'd taken pills for that escape.

The pills were gone. She'd flushed them before she left Boston. She had been tempted to take more than one. And that's when she'd realized she had a problem. Not an addiction, but it could have become one.

The pills had been her crutch. She hadn't dealt with her pain, or her fear, because she'd had that medication to rely on. It had become her way of coping with her unhappiness.

All of it became more clear standing there, facing the stage, facing those same fears.

Alyson turned to face her mother. "This is the end. My final performance as Alyson Anderson. I'm Alyson Forester and after tonight, I'm going home."

And she walked out onstage. When the lights came up and hit her in the face, she was nervous, but not afraid.

She peered out, almost believing Jason would be in the audience. That would be the perfect end to this evening, to see him. But he wasn't there.

And when the concert ended, there were no roses, no notes to tell her he'd see her soon. She told herself it didn't matter. She had made it through this last performance.

No matter what, she was strong.

* * *

Jason walked across his front porch and eased down the steps. He'd had surgery three days before. Not because he had wanted to, but because a horse had pushed him and his knee had finally given up. He hobbled with crutches, wishing he could have at least made it through this night before having the surgery.

Tonight was the fund-raiser for Camp Hope. He shifted the crutches under his arm and headed across the driveway to his truck.

He heard a vehicle slowing to turn into his driveway. He opened his truck door and grabbed the handle above the door to pull himself up into the seat.

Once he got in, he wasn't sure how he would drive.

But it was Beth pulling up next to his truck. So maybe that was one problem solved. She stopped and rolled down the passenger-side window of her truck.

"Where are you going?"

"I'm going to Camp Hope. You wouldn't want to take me, would you?"

She laughed as she got out of her truck. "If I say no, are you really going to try to drive yourself?"

"Yes, I'm going to drive myself."

"I'm not sure what to think about this new Jason Bradshaw."

"What does that mean?" He scooted into the seat, managing to get his left leg in without bumping it on anything.

"It means, scoot over and I'll drive." Beth stood on the running board of the truck, leaning in the driver's side door. "It means that it's about time you lost control and wanted something so badly it's making you a little crazy."

"I don't know what you think I want that's making me crazy."

"You want Alyson Forester back. You want her back more than you ever wanted the world title. You're half crazy thinking she might be at the camp. I don't think she is, but if it'll calm you down a little, I'll take you up there."

"Whatever." But he did want her back. And he was tired of ignoring the fact that her silence was driving him crazy. "Okay, you're right."

"I know. So scoot and I'll drive you."

Jason moved and his sister climbed behind the wheel. She shifted into reverse, turned the wheel and headed down the drive, hitting the road at a speed that made him cringe.

"Could you be a little careful?"

She shot him a look. "Fine, be picky."

"I just put new tires on this thing." He brushed a hand over his face. "I'm sorry."

"Don't mention it, I'm enjoying this. A lot." She laughed and shifted, picking up speed as the tires hummed on the paved road. "So, when you find her, what do you plan on doing? I mean, are you going to do the sweet thing and tell her how much you love her? Or the macho thing—the toss her over your shoulder and elope tactic?"

"I doubt I'll do either."

"Jason, stop trying so hard to hold it together. Stop. Stop. Stop."

"What do you want me to do?"

"Stop being the guy who thinks you always have to control your emotions. Let yourself fall in love and do something crazy."

He smiled at his sister's huge wave of emotion. She'd always been the one willing to jump into love. And his smile faded, because she still had the scars to prove it.

They pulled up the drive to Camp Hope. There were people everywhere, preparing for the charity concert and auction. They still had campers, too. Beth parked and he got out, reaching in the back of the truck for the crutches that he'd need for the next month or so.

They headed up the drive, toward the dining

hall. Jenna saw him and she waved. He nodded and moved in her direction, but she turned and headed toward the stable.

"I guess she doesn't want to talk to you," Beth teased.

"I guess not."

And that's when he heard the piano. And it wasn't the organist from church or one of the campers. He stopped and listened. Beth slipped away. He started to call her back, but she knew better than he did what his emotions were.

Alyson was here. She had come back. Maybe just for this weekend, for the concert, but she was back. And if he had anything to do with it, she would stay.

Even if he had to resort to Beth's macho man tactics.

Timmy and David rushed past him.

"Hey guys, could you do me a favor?"

They put on the brakes and hurried back to his side. And he knew exactly what he needed, and what he was going to do. They accepted the mission he gave them and disappeared into the dining hall, returning a few minutes later with exactly what he'd hoped for.

Alyson played through the song again, preparing for the concert this evening. "It Is Well with My Soul." The song had been Etta's suggestion. She couldn't be here because she was still getting over a bad case of the flu, but she wanted Alyson to play the song for her.

Alyson smiled to herself, thinking back to the previous evening when she'd showed up on Etta's doorstep, surprising her with flowers and the news that she was home for good. Etta had cried. And even Andie had teared up a little.

None of them had mentioned Jason. Alyson hadn't wanted to hear from her sister that she'd been warned not to fall in love with him so she hadn't brought him up. If no one was mentioning him, there had to be a reason.

She played through the song again, embracing the lyrics.

Whatever my lot, thou has taught me to say, it is well, it is well, with my soul.

She closed her eyes and prayed those words would be true and the lyrics would have meaning in her life. She knew that she was where she was meant to be, and no matter what, it would all work out.

Even Jason. She couldn't stop loving him. She'd told herself to let it go. But she couldn't. She loved a cowboy with a Robert Redford smile. And there was a spark of hope in her soul, believing he might even love her.

She closed her eyes and played the song again. "Could you play 'In the Garden'?"

She looked up, and there he was, leaning on metal crutches, watching her. That smile that wouldn't let her sleep at night was on his face. He managed the steps and headed across the stage to where she sat.

"I can play it." She inhaled a deep breath and couldn't let it out when he sat down next to her.

"I would like that." He leaned against her. She realized how much she had missed him. At that moment everything she'd thought she felt for him became very real.

Missing him had ached inside her. Loving him and not knowing what the future held had ached inside her.

She had been so afraid that it would turn out that it was just a summer romance. That fear of losing him had rivaled any stage fright she'd ever felt.

Because at twenty-eight, she finally knew who she was and what she wanted. The idea of him not wanting her back was more than she could think about.

She played his song, closing her eyes, but still aware of him sitting next to her. When she opened her eyes his hand moved from the spot next to the songbook. Something pink and plastic was sitting next to the hymnal.

"What's that?" She reached for it, and immediately knew what it was.

"It's the only ring I could get at the last minute. Shopping in Dawson is limited, you know, and I didn't want to face you empty-handed. I couldn't make it to Vera's or the convenience store to hit the quarter machine. It just so happened that Timmy and David were willing to get this out of the camp treasure box for me."

He took the ring from her hand and slipped it on her pinky finger.

Laughter and love and every other emotion she'd been holding in for days welled up inside her. Alyson wiped away her tears. She held up her hand and admired the plastic ring.

"It's beautiful. Does this mean we're going steady?"

He leaned a little and her breath caught and held. His lips caught hers, gentle, sweet, holding her captive for a long moment as his hands went to her back, keeping her close. It was a familiar place, being in his arms. It felt like forever when he held her like that.

"I couldn't get to Chicago, Alyson. I wanted to be there for you."

"I would have called, but I didn't want to

make you feel as if you had to do something or say something."

"Something like, I love you?" He held her close. "Something like, I want to hold you forever and I'd like to replace that ring on your finger with a real one. Because I want more for us than going steady."

"What do you want?" She touched her forehead to his and waited, because she knew what she wanted.

"I would love to marry you. I'd love to make you Alyson Bradshaw."

"I was kind of planning on being the crazy cat lady living in town and teaching kids to play—"

"No, sorry, I don't think you'll be able to fulfill that role."

"I think you're right. I think I might want Alyson Bradshaw, wife of Jason Bradshaw, more than I want to be single with a dozen cats and a big hat."

"I'm glad to hear that." He kissed her again and again. "Because I think my sister wants me to throw you over my shoulder and elope."

"I think I want the same thing."

Because Alyson Forester loved a cowboy, and now she knew that he loved her back.

"I forgot something." Alyson pulled away

from Jason and when he looked confused, she smiled.

"What did you forget, because I don't know if I can let you leave again."

She touched his cheek and then she leaned toward him, a little breathless as she kissed him, knowing he was hers forever.

"I forgot to tell you that I love you, too," she whispered.

* * * * *

Dear Reader,

Welcome back to Dawson, Oklahoma, to the lives of characters I've come to know. I hope you're enjoying them as much as I am. *The Cowboy's Courtship* is Jason Bradshaw's story, and some of you would say that it is about time he got to be a hero. I think he's always been a hero, but it took time for me to find the right woman for him.

Jason needed a woman in his life who would unlock the secrets of his past and help him to deal with his pain, the pain he's been hiding behind his smile and charm. He needed a woman who would settle him down and keep him in town. That woman happened to be Alyson Anderson, who arrives in Dawson looking for her past.

These two characters don't realize it when they meet, but they have a lot in common. Neither of them has ever really felt connected to another person. Once they meet, that ends for both of them, and the journey of finding themselves and finding love begins.

I hope you enjoy this new book in the cowboy series.

Brenda Minton

QUESTIONS FOR DISCUSSION

1. Alyson chose anger over fear. Why does it sometimes feel easier to control anger than fear? Do both emotions control us equally?

2. Jason Bradshaw's memory issues create several problems for him, including a loss of independence. What would some of the other problems be?

3. Alyson has always seen herself as a person who isn't strong. How does she show that she is stronger than she believed?

4. Camp Hope is a part of the Dawson community. How does it change the people who work there, and what can it do for the children who attend?

5. Andie knew about her sister. Alyson didn't know about Andie. How do you think the two will continue to work through their relationship?

6. Jason has always closed himself off from

emotion, from feeling too much. Why? How did he do this?

7. Alyson figures Jason out by watching him. People tell us more by their actions sometimes than by their words. What does she see in him that maybe others missed?

8. Alyson gradually comes to faith. What is the most important deciding factor in her turning to God?

9. Jason decided early on to build a relationship with Alyson, even though he might not have realized it. He begins to court her. Do you think she realized what he was doing?

10. Alyson has commitments at home in Boston. Is it ralistic to think she would walk away and not go back? What would you do in the same situation?

11. When Alyson leaves, she has dreams of coming back. She makes those dreams about being a cat lady, not about Jason. Why do you think she pushes the dream of Jason from her mind?

12. Jason loves Alyson, so why doesn't he push her to stay? Why doesn't he run after her and bring her back to Dawson?

13. Alyson makes a decision to return to Dawson. She turns away from her career, but she doesn't turn from her family. What allows her to make these decisions?

14. Jason and Alyson share a special bond and have several things in common. How did those things help them understand each other better?

*When his niece unexpectedly arrives at his
Montana ranch, Jules Parrish has no idea
what to do with her—or with Olivia Rose,
the pretty teacher who brought her.
Will they be able to build a life—
and family—together?*

*Here's a sneak peek of
MONTANA ROSE by Cheryl St.John,
one of the touching stories
in the new collection,
TO BE A MOTHER,
available April 2010
from Love Inspired Historical.*

Jules Parrish squinted from beneath his hat
brim, certain the waves of heat were playing
with his eyes. Two females—one a woman,
the other a child—stood as he approached.

The woman walked toward him. Jules dismounted and approached her. "What are you
doing here?"

The woman stopped several feet away.
"Mr. Parrish?"

"Yeah, who are you?"

"I'm Olivia Rose. I was an instructor at the

Hedward Girls Academy." She glanced back over her shoulder at the girl who watched them. "My young charge is Emily Sadler, the daughter of Meriel Sadler."

She had his attention now. He hadn't heard his sister's name in years. *Meriel.*

"The academy was forced to close. I thought Emily should be with family. You're the only family she has, so I brought her to you."

He took off his hat and raked his fingers through dark, wavy hair. "Lady, I spend every waking hour working horses and cows. I sleep in a one-room cabin. I don't know anything about kids—and especially not girls."

"What do you suggest?"

"I don't know. All I know is, she can't stay here."

Will Olivia be able to change Jules's mind and find a home for Emily—and herself?

Find out in
TO BE A MOTHER,
the heartwarming anthology from
Cheryl St.John and Ruth Axtell Morren,
available April 2010
only from Love Inspired Historical.